I0676393

Eclipsia™

Dignity Must Be Returned For All.

Robert P. Francis

&

Joleen Bartles

Eclipsia

Copyright © 2008 by Robert P Francis & Joleen Bartles

All rights reserved. No part of this book, including cover and artwork, may be reproduced or transmitted in any form or by any means without written permission of the authors, except by a reviewer who may quote brief passages in a review.

This book is a work of fiction. Names, characters, places, and incidents are products of the authors' imaginations or are used fictitiously. Any resemblance to actual events or locales or persons living or dead is entirely coincidental.

Revised Edition.

Official website: Eclipsia.net

Contact us at: robertpfrancisjoleenbartles@live.com

Visit LuLu.com

Paperback edition:

ISBN 9780615255132

Library of Congress Control Number: 2008910212

This book is dedicated to all who
suffer under oppression and tyranny.

Acknowledgments

Special thanks to Andrea at Legacy Editing and the editing services at The Write Elements. Thank you to author Victor Milan, who gave us guidance, helpful pointers, and insights into the publishing world. Thank you to Charlotte, who read one of our early rough drafts. Thanks to Arthur C. Clarke, Alan Dean Foster, and a whole host of Science Fiction talents we have read over the years. Special thanks to Gene Roddenberry, George Lucas, and Steven Spielberg, who set all our sights a little higher. Special thanks to Robert J. Brito for your immense support. Also great thanks to Terry, Anne Renee, Jessa, Mildred, Tony, and Nico for your encouragement. Thank you, Judy H., for your English expertise and notes. Thank you, Michelle, Marie, and friends and family. And most importantly, thank you to our wonderful readers.

Preface

Rani peeked out from the branches. He parted some of the leaves, others parted naturally on their own. Brakus might be hiding behind the mound located at the center of the clearing. Or could he be over in the vines? Either way, Rani would find him. They would play together until Talrish hit its peak in the sky. That is when mother said play ended, and you didn't argue with her.

Rani bolted out and made a dash for the mound. Even if Brakus wasn't pressing his body firmly to the ground below it, Rani could look out from the mound's top and see where else his Setiacotion friend might be hiding.

"Brakus! You know I will find you. And when I do . . .." Rani stopped short atop the mound. Something in the sky caught his attention. "What is that?"

The sky had opened up. Something black and hideous was forming gaping holes in the clouds.

Rani stood terrified, his knees giving out from under him.

Brakus noticed, peering from between the vines, that Rani no longer seemed to be playing. Brakus slowly stepped out from his hiding place to join his friend.

"This better not be a trick," Brakus said as he inched forward.

"No," Rani shook his head. "No trick."

Brakus followed Rani's gaze. "What are those?" he asked.

Rani replied, "Whatever they are, they aren't good."

From above, the Lam Warons descended on Eclipsia, bringing with them their insatiable appetites for wealth, power, and control. The thunder of their atmospheric entry hit the Setiacotion's eardrums.

The Lam Waron vessels halted in formation at a very high altitude. Then their giant tailpieces unfurled and pointed toward the planet's surface. Once positioned, they began releasing their poisons. The skies began filling with churning clouds and plumes of yellow smoke.

"Rani! Let's go," Brakus said. He tugged at his friend, removing him slightly from his fixation.

"You're right . . . let's get out of here." Rani said.

The two Setiacotion youths ran for the township.

The smoke continued to thicken, sickening Rani and Brakus. In fact, every living thing became temporarily weakened and more susceptible. Rani and Brakus, along with all of their people, went into an altered state. As the poison surrounded them, they collapsed. They lay vulnerable. They lay fallen.

Amidst the fumes and turmoil, black installations fell from orbit and began taking up operation.

Before coming down to the planet's surface, the Lam Warons cleverly altered their appearances. Under their guises, and immune to their own poisons, they shuttled to the surface. Once below, they appeared before the three higher-brain carrying species: the Remorans, the Kanda, and the Setiacotions.

The Lam Warons enticed them with deceptions. They offered them freedom from worry, life without pain, and endless pleasure. The Lam Warons lured them and they easily took the bait.

While the three species remained under illusions, the Lam Warons uprooted and removed them from the surface. They forced them into the installations and incorporated them into a system. The Remorans, the Kanda, and the Setiacotions immediately lost their connection to the planet and they suffered and atrophied.

Next, the Lam Warons began having Eclipsia stripped of her raw materials. The Lam Warons had the forests decimated and the waters drained and the skies filled with toxic emissions. They stole and hoarded up Eclipsia's resources. Then they had everything they had come for.

Thereafter, Eclipsia remained desolated and ravaged. She was wounded and unable to recuperate, and she remained lost even unto herself.

The Remorans, the Kanda, and the Setiacotions remained incorporated captives shrouded in unceasing gloom and misery ever since. They knew only darkness. It had filled their entire existence. Those unincorporated, if they existed at all anymore, would have to struggle in the shadows.

Four thousand years later, a sole Lam Waron Baron remained. He owned Eclipsia and held control over her.

The planet Eclipsia, robbed of her natural course, remained withering and in a state of sheer environmental collapse. She was located somewhere out beyond Ashton's Belt, beyond even the bridged Sisters of Geridine. She circled in the outermost bounds of the Serendipity, far from the frequented reaches of space.

The Lam Warons had kept Eclipsia a heavily guarded secret. For the ordinary traveler, discovering Eclipsia would be extremely unlikely. Small private transports bypassed the region entirely, having no destinations there. Even an off-the-beaten path vacationer never strayed out quite that far. Neither usually carried enough fuel to manage such a journey. Getting there would be filled with extreme difficulties. The Lam Warons made sure of that. If someone, invited or not, happened to uncover something unusual, they did not normally live to tell about it.

Most who resided out in the vastly populated consumer worlds of the Serendipity had enjoyable lives. Now and again, a few of them heard rumors of the existence of Eclipsia. They were unaware of the atrocities being committed on Eclipsia on their behalf. Tales circulated, filled with fanciful speculation and only the slightest hint of fact. Eclipsia remained a mere rumor.

The consumer worlds went about living in an ignorant bliss, unaware of what the future held in store for them.

Only the pitiful light of Eclipsia's moon cast natural definition to the cold and formidable landscape. At certain vantage points, another source gave off illumination, albeit, of a very unnerving sort.

Massive processing facilities were now scattered over most of Eclipsia. Covering miles, they rose in clusters on her dark surface. From above, they looked like cancerous growths. Towers mushroomed and loomed high above. Tubes formed vast connectways, and centers teeming with activity confined two of the incorporated species. They emitted an eerie, flickering, blue luminance. The electrified flashes of light from those dungeons of servitude could prevent a nasty foot-lock in a crevice or a dangerous slide down a chasm. However, it was not possible for the three species to be outside. In over four thousand years, no one had walked the land.

The Breach

Axreal belonged to the Setiacotions. Like all of her incorporated species, she suffered from the changes the Lam Warons had forced upon them. They had more than their fair share of maladies and diseases.

The Setiacotions ailed from stunted growth, and deformities on different levels. They had very short and stressful existences. They suffered afflictions due to the manipulative nature of the labors in the Lam Waron processing facilities. Like trapped seedlings unable to germinate, the Setiacotions existed buried under immense burdens. They never saw themselves apart from The System that bound and controlled them. They labored. That was all they knew, that was all they could be allowed to know.

The stress of a labor-intensive existence periodically built up in Axreal, and she underwent seizures. In this way, for brief moments she left the onslaught of labors. However, doing so could have robbed her of her life on many occasions. Little by little, however, she gained some control over them.

Ooohhh . . . it . . . is happening again, she thought as she began to undergo a most intense seizure.

As she sat, a rumbling jolt moved up her spine, causing her body to spasm. Her arms trembled violently out in front of her. Then her entire body shook. It began. A hundred thousand vibrations. Axreal blurred into the background, left behind was an afterimage. A ghost. Vanishment. The Breach.

Everything had dissolved and given way. She found herself, for the first time, transported elsewhere. She rose and stood up with wide-eyed astonishment. She felt the air rush into her lungs. Her numbed mind strained to take in the overloading messages it received: the colors, the temperature, and the breeze. Everything appeared blurry and distorted. A constant existence spent in miserable hard work and forced self-neglect had clouded her sight.

"Where am I? Where is the ceiling? Where did my workstation go? What am I standing on?" Axreal panicked and could not refrain from speaking aloud. "What's happening to me?"

She looked down. *That is odd.* The ground was vibrating and she along with it. Tiny rocks rolled about her feet and scurried atop the hard surface on which she stood. The rumbling activity from inside her previous world shook the crust in her proximity like a quake. Her first escape out onto the surface of Eclipsia had been terrifying.

"What is going to be the punishment for this, why is this happening?"

Axreal said while nervously pulling on a strand of her dingy blond hair.

Prior to this, The System predetermined almost all of Axreal's actions. It programmed and shuttled her from duty to duty, never allowing her any rest. The demands made on it never ended, so it never allowed her to stop, either. If she deviated from its instructions, The System would reduce her artificial food rations. Worse yet, it would douse her with chemical poisons to keep her dulled and compliant.

Axreal trembled. *This cannot be happening. This is not real.* Her eyes darted in every direction. She was overwhelmed. Then she went into a seizure and it returned her. She vanished back into the confinement of the processing facilities. She looked about her podule. *Everything is the same. It appears The System doesn't know that I ever left.*

Over the next work interval, she took chances when she could to replay her recent journey. The strange sights and sensations continued to puzzle her.

What was that place? Could it be some strange part of the processing facilities? What purpose could it possibly serve? Her fear gave way to her surmounting questions and curiosity overwhelmed her. *I need answers*, she thought. *I must try to return.*

Eventually, she found an appropriate time, alone within her podule, to initiate a seizure and she went through the breach again. On coming out, this time, she noticed her focus had improved. All around her, she saw the strange, dark purple formations and the swirling overhead vapors. Now, at a few paces in front of her, she saw what appeared to be a male of her species. Awed by the sight, she approached him slowly. She tried to gather as much information about him as she could, before she made herself known to him.

What could he possibly be doing here?

He had good looks for a male Setiacotion, unbeknownst to him or anyone. Personal appearance had little value. Only things related to production mattered. Hence, Jerish's attractiveness: his dark hair, thick brows, and masculine features held no significance, until, perhaps, now.

Axreal examined him. This was the closest she had ever been to one of her own kind. *He is worn and tired, like me. He looks dizzy, disoriented. He is covered in the same grime, too.* Jerish rubbed his eyes in an attempt to clear them. He removed his hands from his face revealing his smoky blue eyes, which peered out from their dark recesses. It was very evident that he had been horribly mistreated.

Axreal spoke to him, "The System keeps us divided . . . none of us are ever allowed to be this close. We rarely get to speak directly."

"You are right. It is strange to be talking, like this, to each other. What has happened, and where are we?" he said, trembling in the cold.

"Somehow we left. Wherever this place is, it does not appear at all like the processing facilities. I have been here once before though."

"You have?" he said in amazement.

"Yes, but I did not stay very long." Then she proceeded to yank her fatigue collar down over her shoulder. "Look at this," she told him.

The System had burned a brand into her flesh during her early development. Her fingers traced the symbols, which formed from her scars. She recalled the incident being a violation, and that the strange alien symbols held some importance. From them she sounded out the recognizable characters and she pronounced her name.

"I am Axreal 45."

"Axreal 45, it is agreeable to meet you. What if I just call you Axreal?"

"That is fine."

"Whul, I have a name for myself also. I call myself Jerish. I have scars like that. But, that's not where I got my name. One time I saw something unusual being made. It was some type of minicar, like for a child. They put a lot of work and detail into making it. The label read, 'For my dearest Jerish'. I thought whoever that was, he had to have been someone special. And so I took that name for myself."

"It is agreeable to meet you, Jerish," said Axreal. "How many cycles are you?"

"I am twelve cycles," he replied.

"We are close in age," she said, while brushing her hair to the side.

"Why is your arm like that?" he asked.

Axreal turned her head to the side, not wanting to look at the surface of her right arm as she raised it upward. Something unnatural loomed under the skin.

"I was at my workstation, during a long period of labor. A new procedure failed to recognize everything I needed to do to carry out its tasks. I didn't respond fast enough." Axreal pressed her long lashes shut. "The mechanism took apart my arm."

Axreal barely survived this ordeal. For its remedy, The System agreed to have her surgically outfitted with a retractable-mechanized arm. The System had Axreal's arm created, not out of any sympathy or concern for her well-being. Rather, it was advantageous for The System to do so.

"They made me so that I could carry out even more tasks. They made me able to work around conditions like the one that took my arm apart to begin with. I became more useful, more dexterous. If they hadn't outfitted me with this, The System would have disposed of me."

Jerish did not want to cause Axreal any further grief, so he asked, "Can we have a look around?"

"I think it is safe to take a short look," she replied.

"What is this place for?" Jerish asked.

"I do not know. It is not like anywhere else I have ever been."

Getting used to maneuvering by way of the ground took some practice. They took careful steps until they got more comfortable. They circled around for a while.

"What do you suppose that is over there?" He pointed toward a dim sphere above.

"I have never seen anything like that before either," she remarked. "How strange."

Both wondered what might lie over and beyond what they had managed to see. Given so much to explore, they would need to come here another time.

"It would probably be best to go back now," Axreal said after observing additional unexplainable sights.

"How?" responded Jerish.

"I reentered the breach," she said. She saw his face and immediately sensed his puzzlement. "The passageway that opens now during my seizures."

"How am I supposed to get back then?"

"Let's see, is this about where you first appeared?" she asked.

"Yes, I think so," Jerish said while gathering his bearings.

"Do you recall what was going on exactly, before you left?"

"Whul, yes, I was alone in my podule," he said. After a momentary hesitation he spoke, "I got frustrated and had one of my tantrums. I have them regularly. Usually I can control them. This time was intense though. Thoughts raced with each other in my mind. Then I started spinning. I hit my head once so I placed my arms out to my sides. Before I knew it I was spinning so fast, I had been lifted away. When I came back to normal, I found myself here. Then you showed up."

"That is somewhat like what I went through, but I shook so much that it caused me to leave." Then Axreal asked Jerish, "Can you do it over again?"

"I can try," he began to recall his tantrums and to muster the tensions. "This will work, right?" he wondered aloud.

"We will find out. It, so far, has worked for me," Axreal spoke. "Then," she proposed, "Maybe we can return here?"

"Sure, I'd like that," he replied.

"I was in my main compartment during my podule's inactive mode when I left. Was your podule in inactive mode also?" she asked.

"Yes," Jerish replied.

"Good, then we are available at the same times to try to return here. I want to know what this place is for," Axreal said.

"It's got me wondering too," said Jerish.

"As long as we don't get found out," Axreal replied.

"If we do, I probably won't receive any rations," Jerish said.

"I am sure it'll be far worse than that, for both of us," Axreal spoke. "If all goes well, we will be able to see each other again. If not, it was agreeable to have met you."

"I will look forward to meeting you again Axreal," Jerish then stood where he first appeared.

He readied himself and did, in fact, return. Axreal watched as Jerish vanished. The sight shocked her. No longer was she naive of what it looked like. Minute feelings of sadness and sympathy formed inside her.

I don't think we are supposed to be coming here, Axreal thought. *Something could go wrong. We could lose the ability to return. What if our schedules change? What if The System finds out?*

Axreal briefly set aside her fears so she could make herself ready to return. The molten rock, dark sky, and cool night air shook away into a blur. She found herself returned to her habitat podule.

The Remains

After intervals of extensive harsh labors, Axreal and Jerish reunited. A rain had dampened the dark Eclipsian surface. A rapid breeze blew and the night air grew brisk.

"I am relieved you made it," Axreal said.

Their faces came in and out of sight, due to the flashes of blue factory light flickering across them.

"Me too, I am grateful it worked," Jerish said. He firmly dug his right shoe into the ground, testing the rock and soil surface. "I wasn't sure I'd ever get to see you again."

"Me either, we are fortunate. What direction do you think we should go in?" Axreal asked. The whites of her eyes stood out from her grimy complexion and the dark terrain.

"Whul, this looks the most interesting," he said. For a brief moment, out of Axreal's notice, he extended his arm off to one side. His fingers rotated back and forth in curiosity about the breeze.

"There were pits and lots of loose rocks, remember?" she replied. "That's not going to be safe."

"Oh yeah, you're right, whul we better try somewhere else then," Jerish said. "Here, hold tight, let's go this way."

They moved forward when the flashes of blue factory light permitted.

"It's slippery—Jerish. Wait a minute," Axreal said as she mechanically held back strands of her hair. Her blonde ringlets blew wildly in the breeze. "I can't see where we're going."

"Keep steady, right here is okay," he said while guiding her.

"Let's wait for the next big flash," Axreal said.

A song spun its way through the porous rocks and battered canyon. It flew as if carried on ribbons, which interwove the entire area. It caught up to Jerish and Axreal where it resonated off the damp terrain. From the stars overhead to the under soles of their feet, the melody surrounded them. The words beckoned forth in an astral melody.

Far and beyond wondrous realities, lay ahead for you. Imagine all is within your grasp. You can accomplish more than you can possibly conceive, Far and beyond wondrous . . .

Had Jerish had a heart, it might have resonated there, perhaps been set aflame there. Yet Jerish did not have a heart, nor did Axreal, nor for that matter did any of the servile denizens of Eclipsia. They had perhaps the organ that pumped blood through their veins and arteries. However, as for passion, of any kind, The System had long ago stamped it out.

"Do you hear that?" exclaimed Jerish. He harkened up to one of Axreal's windblown ears. "There and over there!" The coarse fiber of Jerish's grey and dingy work fatigues restricted his movement as he frantically pointed.

"What are you talking about?" Axreal asked.

Jerish heard a faint wind chiming melody. "It sounds like someone."

"Are you sure? Maybe it's the air?"

"No. I don't think so."

"We haven't seen anyone else out here." Axreal tried to maintain her balance. She had not heard it.

"Whul it seems to have stopped now anyways," he said.

"We should get through this area and then start heading back," Axreal spoke in a low voice just in case there was someone or something around. It would be best to remain cautious. They had not yet learned enough about their strange surroundings.

They decided to return for now, recalling landmarks they had passed to indicate the way back to the spot where they would breach.

After a number of labor-intensive intervals, they went out exploring once again. Each time, they noticed, their minds began to clear and their bodies felt somehow revived. They briefly experienced a respite from the pain and monotony of the labors. Being outside lifted a level of their griminess and some of their gloom. They gained a degree of vitality.

After a long strenuous hike, finding much the same, Jerish tried to be encouraging. "We need to make it to at least those," he said, motioning toward an outcropping of ridges. They drew his attention because of the intriguing way they rose up vertically. Their summits appeared to undulate where they met the horizon.

"Maybe so we don't get lost, let's mark our way," Axreal said. Her face appeared to glow in a subtle, healthier hue.

Jerish replied, "Sure, good idea. I know what we can do. Help me turn these over." He then lifted a cluster of magma formations leaving behind an obvious impression.

"We should get moving. Inactive mode will soon be over. I don't want to find out what happens if we are discovered missing or late," Axreal said. "It's getting close."

Jerish tried to coax Axreal. "Don't worry so much, we still have awhile yet, let's see what else there is. I want to see if I can hear that song again." Something shown white in the corner of his eye. "Look!" he blurted out as they continued walking along. "What are these? There are more over here."

Alabaster bits and pieces of something rested sparsely before them. Some of the fragments they discovered strewn about or encased in the molten rocks. Others formed small mounds.

Axreal lifted a few and attempted to join them, "These fit together. They are components of something."

The broken bits and pieces, in actuality, once belonged to living animals. An abundance of aquatic animal bones meant that the area had at one time held water.

Four millennia ago, some of the land animals had amassed here seeking refuge. They attempted to relieve their agony from the intense heat of the blasts, caused by the Lam Waron detonations, which melted the land. After which the Lam Warons expected all remaining unincorporated species to no longer exist.

An entire field of their remains lay scattered ahead. Axreal involved herself with attempting to solve this mystery and she went off in search for more of the fragments.

Jerish remarked, "I have never seen anything like this!"

He raised one up quizzically to his nostrils to see if it also had a scent. Rotating it around, he examined its sides. He looked up and then he handed it out towards her, but Axreal was nowhere to be seen.

A swelling sensation rose up within him, an awareness he had never felt before. Shocked, he let the fossil fall from his hands and he clutched his chest. He did so for having lost Axreal and for the alarming discovery of being utterly alone in a place he knew little about.

Unsure what to do next, Jerish called out for her, "Axreal." When this provided no response, he cupped his hands about his mouth and began hollering, "Axreal! Axxxreaaaall!"

Panic-stricken, Jerish became aware of what he might lose. He did not want their emerging friendship cut short when new possibilities had just begun to present themselves. Coming here and being with Axreal gave him something to look forward to. He had never had that before.

For an instant it occurred to him, "Did she breach back? Oh, wait that's not possible we are too far out and why would she attempt to do it here?"

Frantically looking about, Jerish stopped. A billow of dust formed ahead. This area was a dry, flat wash, so Jerish did not wait for the electrified flashes of factory light to proceed. Neither had Axreal. She had been less cautious than normal and she had landed on her haunches at the base of a powdery twenty-foot slope.

"Help, Jerish, I'm down here!" Axreal exclaimed while looking at herself. Her fatigues were full of dirt and snags. A grey, ash-like powder covered her. Grit had somehow made its way into the grooves of her mechanical arm. It threatened malfunction.

On hearing Axreal's reply, Jerish said, "Whew, I thought I lost you. We need to stay together." He proceeded to slide down alongside her. Dirt collected in the cuffs of his pant legs. "That'll teach you to go off when there isn't enough light. I thought I had lost you for good. I even felt something strange happen inside me!" He scolded her reminiscent of Axreal's own authoritative tone. "What made you wander off, anyway?"

"I thought I saw some sort of head. It was staring right at me, and on its face it had the openings for a pair of eyes but there was nothing in them. So then I went a little further to check it out. And then what I was standing on, up there, gave way." Axreal spoke as she looked back up the incline briefly. She had seen a good-sized, intact skull bone. She only caught a brief glimpse of it. It frightened her. Had it really been there or not?

Jerish shivered, "Are you okay, and whul, where did it go?"

"I'm not sure. Perhaps whatever I thought I saw really wasn't there at all. I am fine. Just covered in dirt," Axreal said.

"That makes two of us," he said as he crinkled his thick brows, giving her a wink with a quirky grin.

At seeing his expression, Axreal let out a tiny giggle.

"What was that?" asked Jerish.

"I don't know."

"I have never heard you do that before."

"I have never had any reason to."

Jerish got back on his feet while offering out his hand to her. "Here let me help you up."

While regaining her balance, Axreal said, "I wonder why this is happening to us, and we still have no idea what this place is for and what purpose . . ."

Their hands remained clasped. They had learned doing so served as a support in balancing, and grasping each other in this way proved helpful while maneuvering the terrain. Axreal and Jerish often held hands.

"All this open space in which to roam, all this going off wherever we choose, I wish it could always be like this," he said.

"One thing I know for certain is that there are a lot of things we weren't told about and . . ." Axreal said.

Jerish cut in, "We have been purposefully kept away from here for some reason. We *should* try to find out why."

Axreal did not like being interrupted. "I suppose The System couldn't control us for its purposes if we could merely choose where and when to go. None of us would choose to be back there," she said.

"Perhaps it *can* always be like this," he offered. "Why don't we just stay?"

"Don't mistake me, I would choose to never go back also." Axreal pursed her pale yellow lips together. She noticed more of the wear and tear of factory life was being stripped away. "But we better first make sure if we can survive out here. I do not think we know enough about it. I don't know if there are any rations. I do know it is a little easier to breathe out here. I am more conscious, more aware of things. It does feel better to be here."

"I feel better also. And I like making choices for ourselves like we are able to do here, and I like when we get together." Jerish nodded in the direction of the processing facilities. "There is nothing for us back there. I hate what we are made to do!"

"I don't like it there, either," said Axreal. "Here…in this place, we have gotten better."

They continued brushing off the dirt. Axreal shook the artificial arm forcefully, releasing the accumulated grit, thinking all the while that when the time was right they would flee.

"We need to learn a few more things about this place before we can decide to remain," she said, attempting to convince Jerish.

Jerish did not want to leave. He slid a tiny fossil bone into his shirtsleeve pocket. He did not know exactly what it was. However, it would serve to remind him, while back in confinement, of this place and their adventures in it. This was the only happiness he had ever known. Once back to the throes of labor, consciousness sometimes got lost or taken, and along with it some memories and awareness. Jerish might think that maybe it was all a dream, somehow unreal. The fossil would serve as a reminder.

They made the trek back along the impressions they left in the ground while also planning their next breach. Fear, hunger, and the possibility of punishment called them to retreat again.

The Loathsome CreXan

A towering complex stood within the center of the processing facilities. Within it was the control hub. CreXan transmitted his orders to the hub via his interface aboard his immense Resort Haven. From the hub, orders went out to the processing facilities. Tendrils of wiring snaked throughout the complex. Signals broadcast by microwaves to receptor sites, fed instructions to the incorporated three species who labored the mammoth factories and staffed CreXan's lair.

Within the processing facilities, the air contained substances that controlled behavior and regulated biological activity. The System removed life and freedom from the incorporated species by this and other means. Their programming and harsh treatment left them subservient, docile, stolen from, deprived of self, and without free will. Their sole purpose was to labor; that was all the existence they knew. That was all they could be allowed to know.

CreXan was a Lam Waron, low to the ground. His rippled, chelatenous back supported him when he arched to pose his long, transparent bulk upright. Every heinous act resulted in an added layer to his hardened purple coating. Having grown so long, it now could protrude over his sides serving as further armor. He had three different colored appendages below and two in the front. His sides contained fluid-filled pink and brown nodules. Two large honed fangs hid beneath folds of flesh. He leered forward through tiny, slitted eyes, making him appear condescending. A pungent odor of decay lingered about him, his voice a high-pitched squeal.

CreXan never had to see his "handiwork". He never had to make any effort, even for his own care. Certainly, he never had to be in contact with all but a select few of the millions of his slaves. Not seeing or knowing the slaves made it easier to treat them as objects instead of as living beings. It was easy then to make brash decisions in total disregard of their well-being. He had altogether forgotten they had life. His agenda was all that mattered. He never had to witness the vast resources plundered from Eclipsia under his authority.

He had no remorse for his actions, only the acquisition of power mattered. Totally acquiring the Lam Waron operations and capturing all for himself was the game he had played against the other Barons. It was a game of *last one standing*. In pursuit of this goal, the Lam Warons had decimated their entire race, all except for the five, and destroyed many a world in the process.

CreXan's Resort Haven, an immense city laid out on a gigantic hovering disk, lay sheltered and hidden, miles away from the nearest processing facility, across mined craters, barren mountain ranges, and suspended above an acid filled dead sea. Tucked away within the Resort Haven, he kept himself hidden to all but a few.

Eclipsia existed far from his origins. Yet all served him, it did not hurt to have them know of nothing else but The System and its orders, toils, and demands. They had no way of knowing that their lives belonged to him. He gave them purpose in the myriad of blind repetitive tasks he programmed them to follow. One day they might mine for ore, sew clothing, fasten motherboards, form chemical compounds, or package freight for the great distribution platforms. They may labor at all, none, or each of these in a day's cycle. At their workstations, the Setiacotions carried out the endless dictates of The System. They appeared like legions of puppets jerked by strings, pale, emotionless, deformed, and nearly indecipherable from the mechanizations that incorporated them into The System. Day and night, they manufactured goods for the Serendipity, the entire known universe. Day and night, they churned out endless wealth for CreXan.

The Lam Warons, thousands of years ago, offered irresistible bait to the three species. Once they took the bait, the Lam Warons pulled them violently from their original habitat and switched them into laboring in the manufacturing facilities. The System ensnarled them. Charmed with false images, each slave was misled and separated from knowing each other. They were lied to. All were unable to form correctly into the beings they were designed to be. They no longer resembled what they once were. They were now the pawns of CreXan, upon which he harvested his great fortunes.

Eclipsia was not the first world the Lam Warons had subjugated and pillaged, nor would it be their last. They had roamed the Serendipity in the great woven designed Harvester Ships. Lying down upon a planet, they would then reshape it into their hideous designs, and carry out their mal-intentions.

The Lam Warons recorded their observations of Eclipsia's three higher-brain carriers during their incorporation process. These records remained buried under volumes of ancient data stored in a vault in CreXan's Haven. It told of a secret knowledge. It described that under the conditions they wrought, hearts did not form and deprivation caused other characteristics and abilities to become dormant, recede, or simply never develop. It told that the three species without contact with their natural world became malformed, stunted, and weak. They became sickly, devoid of mind, body, and spirit, dwarfed and atrophied. Without the natural fresh air, sunlight, and waters, their life energy depleted. Taken off the surface, separated from the rest of the organisms, they could not properly develop. Weakened, they were easily led.

The records told that it was imperative to keep them on low artificial rations and to never let them eat of the natural vegetation. The natural organic foods that had once grown in abundance on the planet's surface were healthy and much too potent to let them have. Certain characteristics depended upon their consumption to manifest.

Part of the secret knowledge was to deprive them of their freedom and they became the Lam Waron's to do with as they pleased. It was for that reason the Lam Warons contained the Setiacotions, the Kanda, and the Remorans. The Lam Warons rounded them together and picked them up off the surface. They also made them expand the processing facilities. Once enslaved inside the factories or the Resort Haven, they then had no means by which to escape. If any obtained their freedom, they would be a great threat to CreXan.

Since the Lam Warons arrived on Eclipsia, they little by little dwindled in remaining numbers. Quarreling and fighting amongst each other, the Lam Warons did themselves in. A series of detonations altered the planet's atmosphere, interfered with the planet's axis, and slowed its speed around Talrish, its sun.

"The vacuum craft are ready to transport for resource gathering on Urxis Minor. All is proceeding well. Now all I have to do is make ready my plans for the Baron's Wamp Agglomeration, the gathering of the prevailing diadems. On my trip, perhaps I can stop over for a little entertainment; maybe cheat at a little gambling at Arckael 3. Riches always find their way back to me. Eeehhh, now about eliminating the other Barons…with the others gone I will be able to reign supreme. Finally, I will be THE LAST. I will possess all, I will own everything!" he arrogantly boasted.

CreXan slithered back into his leather sofa. Everything in his Resort Haven, from the adornments, candles, and artwork, was formed through someone's suffering. With one of his long talons, he picked off some of his pink and brown nodules and consumed them, smug in the knowledge that he amongst the five would catapult to the top. For he alone demonstrated the greatest prowess, cunning, and keen manipulation.

When all of Eclipsia's resources were used up, and when CreXan so decided, he could then move. He had already isolated a suitable and vulnerable new world on which to relocate. The harvesting of new slaves and construction of new factories would have to be further underway, though. His hovering Resort could lift off and temporarily merge with a redistributor ship, which would deliver it to the next planet slated for occupation.

He planned, when that day came, to dispose of the Setiacotion, Remoran, and Kanda slaves, except for those utilized for the relocation process, and self-destruct the Eclipsian manufacturing installations. Forever she would remain an uninhabitable wasteland. Once Eclipsia was completely depleted, CreXan could then cast her off like a chunk of useless stone. She would be forever lost. She would be void of all life.

"I will take everything from this rock!" he squealed to himself while smiling and catching a glorious sight of himself in one of his multitude of intricately designed mirrors. This particular one allowed him to see himself from different vantage points. An ornate framework lay across the face. CreXan looked deep into his own eyes and said, "I have exceeded my predecessors and I will also eliminate my rival brethren!"

He rose up on his appendages to scurry along the gaudy corridor leading to the antechamber to his suite. The Kanda, alerted to his intentions, madly rushed to prepare his quarters for their master's arrival. The towels were folded, his robes neatly hung and arranged, fresh linens were laid out. The Citmop, a delicate velvety multilayered cake of the finest Lam Waron cuisine was prepared and waiting on his golden bedroom platter for him to delight in. The platter had upturned, convoluted and twisted sides, predominately gold, with green and blue bands speckled in maroon; it curved to accommodate CreXan's scooping talon.

The brawny Kanda doorman opened the suite's chamber doors. CreXan entered the room, his segmented torso moving side to side, his slitted eyes looking about in anticipation of the Citmop.

"BRING FORTH UNTO ME MY CITMOP," his squealing voice demanded as his fangs protruded.

Certain Kanda youths received training solely just to become his Resort chefs. Some youths' existences centered on preparation for other specific duties. For example, an entire class of Kanda studied just to attend to CreXan's medical needs. They knew little of their own physiology and suffered for it. There own well-being was not to be focused on, only that of CreXan mattered. For the Kanda to focus on themselves meant being less prepared to serve CreXan at any given time. It would be like stealing from the master. The System did not keep defective Kanda around long enough for CreXan to notice usually.

Turning to his chief Kanda drudge, CreXan said, "Do you think I am overweight Lorese?" CreXan eyed his graceful servant. She was mottled, pocked, and lanky, which fit the profile of her race. Her firm, thin body and piercing aquamarine eyes stood out as exceptional. The System found the Kanda to be less physically adept, so it used them for Resort duties. As chief drudge, Lorese was programmed to dust CreXan's inner chambers, polish his collections, and oversee CreXan's other personal drudges. She alone was allowed some liberty. One of her main functions was to remind the tyrant of his glory. She also had the duty to boost his ego. Above everything else, she must always AGREE.

"You have done so much for us, you are so beautiful, and your mighty deeds are known throughout all of the Serendipity." All the while, she thought to herself, *How pathetic, you are nothing but a leech, why I have to spend all my time doing things for you is insanity, how I would love to cut your head off and throw your body into the sea!*

Engrossed and mesmerized by Lorese's physical appearance, CreXan reached to touch her cheek. He caressed it, his nails curled around her chin. *Maybe*, he thought to himself. Then CreXan said, "When the time comes to relocate to the new planet, I will take you with me."

Lorese replied, "I will look forward to it." She thought instead, *I'd rather die, you vile, nasty creature. What makes you think I'd really want to go anywhere with you, let alone to another planet?*

CreXan continued thinking to himself, *But alas, I won't need you.*

CreXan, with the use of his glance, commanded a transparent display to appear before him. It erected in mid-air. Through the interface, he accessed The System. He entered his password. On occasion, he signaled it to provide extra rations for Lorese. He liked her voice and he liked to gaze upon her. It did not hurt the way her textured dress revealed the outline of her hindquarters. It was for that reason that she was uniquely qualified and chosen for this role.

"Let me see," he said, scrolling through options. He clicked his way across the menu, from assigning the use of cheaper materials to be used in a certain line of manufactured goods, the consumers would need to go through more of them and he could then increase consumption. He sent out word of new procedures he wanted implemented; he remarked aloud resolving one, "The XCVJ components are no longer viable, orders have been down for cycles, those facilities need to be shutdown and the slaves disposed of." In addition, he fashioned a communiqué regarding the Wamp Agglomeration, the gathering of the Barons, which included a request for the itinerary. Once he knew all that was planned, he could get Lorese to pack the appropriate personal effects. For thirteen intervals he would be gone, all the while making sure, he kept his standing.

"Not to worry," CreXan thought aloud to himself. He juggled a small artifact, a mere trinket. Perhaps it was the last remains of a once thriving civilization. "The System will continue to function while I am gone. Oh, lest I forget…" He ordered the machine, saying, "one additional supply of rations for Lorese, now remove the equivalent from the weakest performing Setiacotion. I think I will retire." He yelled, "Lorese prepare my comforters. The ornate vaulted ceilings echoed with his discharge, and orders. "I'mmm hungry!"

"Yes Your Magnificence. I'll be back quickly with a snack," said Lorese.

"Hurry it up!"

Lorese yelled back to the drudges on her way out, "You and you assist CreXan into the Great Bath."

A gentle waterfall began to pour fragrant suds over him. It was not enough to mask his foul odor. Incense burned in the corners, which made CreXan's odor more tolerable to him. His new delicacies arrived on other fanciful platters for his never-ending cravings. An extensive massage and mud treatment helped to keep him comfortable. He would need those for as long as the occupation of Eclipsia lasted, as his alien body had never grown completely acclimated.

Lorese always outwardly complied. Her animosity did take physical form, however inconspicuously. Whenever having to give in to his demands, she would push her shoulders forward, straighten her arms with elbows locked, and intertwine her fingers in a handclasp. Outwardly, she always appeared eager, obedient, and efficient. In this manner, she had CreXan fooled. In her tightly gripped hands, she barely contained her hate; in the jumping up and down of her thumbs, she barely contained her frustrations.

Kanda did not suffer the same strife and hardships as the other incorporated species because they resided mainly in the Resort Haven. Existing in stark contrast were the daily routines endured by the Setiacotions. They suffered hunger, abuse, experimentation, and torture. Many would not survive this day's workload. Their bodies were thrown into great heaps, and some were scraped off workstations where exhaustion, age, or infirmity had caught up to them.

Existence in the Factory

The System controlled the development of three main species. Axreal and Jerish like their entire race, started infancy in incubators at the Remoran nursery. The Remorans utilized Setiacotion and Kanda genetic material, stored here, to develop offspring. Having never experienced a mother's love they developed artificially. The Remorans, however, took steps to ensure that their own means of developing offspring remained closer to normal.

The System programmed the three species with what they needed to know. It informed them extensively of what would pertain to carrying out its orders. The System made them to fit all of its purposes. To its great advantage, The System kept them ignorant, even about themselves.

Setiacotions remained at the nursery until they matured enough for The System to outfit them with a podule. The podules measured nearly twenty feet from the base to the top, and they were twenty feet in diameter. Receptors dotted the exterior. Color coded nodes encircled the outside where occasionally different connective feeds plugged into them. The largest of these fed electricity to power the orb. Transparent sections in odd contorted shapes served like windows from the varying levels. From this dire view, the occupant saw only stagnation, repetition, and mechanizations. Inside the dismal confines and compartments, a slave could find only a few of his or her most rudimentary needs installed or recycled within.

Axreal returned to her standard size podule and regretted being back. She had but just a short while remaining. She opened a small, odd-shaped storage compartment embedded in the podule's wall. She pried loose a wall segment, revealing a hiding place, which she had secretly formed.

"There you are. I told you I wouldn't be gone long."

She reached within and pulled out an oddly constructed doll. Close examination revealed that it was composed of residual manufacturing components, like scraps of foam, fibers, shreds, little items very much like lint, which went unnoticed by The System. Over time, she had managed to hide these away. She had compressed them together crudely into arms, legs, a body and a head. A small bit of the filling came loose, and she quickly pressed it back into place. She gave the doll a sort of hug, and then placed it back.

Stale air blew and bio-altering gasses constantly assaulted her. For the majority of The System's demands, it would douse her with various gasses. One of the gasses worked all of the time preventing normal natural sleep.

The stark, ugly, and dour confines of the podule kept her assailed in a horrific alien design. She pushed her body and placed it in odd positions to be able to move her way between the slanted angles and contortions. The confining walls and small cramped compartments caused Axreal to scream internally, *I'm claustrophobic. I need out of here, this is disgusting!* She thought aloud, "Ooh my head hurts . . . I can't breathe well."

The System then prompted her. She obeyed as if hypnotized. She crawled up into a tube, just as she had thousands of times before.

Only this time when she complied saying, "I won't forget. You can't have my memories."

She entered the Cerebral Infuser. While deep in rapid eye movement, the C.I. confiscated her mind, filling it with hypnotic virtual reality, thereby installing her programming. Once The System completed her instructions, it began to rouse Axreal. The System's programming released a gas into the air within the cell, thereby awakening her.

Once jolted from her cell, Axreal sped mindlessly through the hygiene and dress regiments. She stepped into a stall, placed her feet apart onto the foot contours and raised her arms above her head, a ritual surrender to the inevitable. Air scoured her sensitive skin. She never felt fully clean. She rushed to place her neglected body into her fatigues. Then she forced down her repugnant allotment of food rations, while the podule traveled at super high velocity.

The podule screeched, vibrated and shook vigorously. Axreal was not distracted by the thunderous echoing clamor made by the podule as it raced down the connectways. Once at her assigned destination, the podule quartered her off into her workstation. Axreal got into ready position. Instructions commanded her into a multitude of pain-ridden mandates. For fear of painfully losing her life, she exacted all of them out.

The Lam Warons integrated the Setiacotions into the processing facilities so well that it was difficult to tell where the person ended and the machine began. Each slave toiled within, spending the majority of his or her duration inside his or her podule, much in the way a snail carries around its home on its back.

At some junctures, huge greased docking rod apparatuses interlocked multiple podules into a symmetrical matrix, resembling a DNA helix. Podules made their way around spiraling tracks and highways. Screeching and clamoring, they grouped together to coordinate for their tasks and readjusted for others.

Connectways ran along factory installations, including maintenance depots, communication relays, and refueling ports. Power plants, raw material storages, construction sites, computer hubs, waste removal, ration procurement, and the massive engines that drove The System lay dispersed throughout. The intense energies and activities illuminated the Eclipsian skies with eerie blue flashes and an unsettling atmosphere.

The System shipped goods and merchandise to the consumer worlds via the dockyards that resided in the mushrooming hundred level towers. Vacuum craft collected habitat podules to transport the slaves to outlying planets. There they gathered and mined for raw materials from new sources to be brought back and utilized. CreXan recently had The System devise this new fleet of craft to make transporting slaves quicker and to utilize off-world facilities more efficiently.

At set intervals, the podules required maintenance and The System powered them down. It was for this reason that the Setiacotions got some rest. It was a consequence of the machines needing to be maintained. When in their inactive mode, the podules stayed stored like eggs in a crate in the great Setiacotion dormitories. They rested there, by the thousands, parked idle in row after row, awaiting computer instructions. After inactive mode, gigantic arms selected and hoisted up the podules and deposited them into slick tubes where they were whisked away for another long duration of strenuous and crippling toils.

As sophisticated, extensive, and elaborate as The System was, it still relied on the labor, abilities, intelligence, and the training of living organisms. All processes flowed together smoothly, so from CreXan's point of view, all he had to do was put in a request and the result was carried out. Nothing could be easier.

Torbot and His Colony

Dawn broke as Talrish ascended. Torbot sprang from rock to rock, his sticky gel-like arms would catch a hold then slingshot him to his next location. He had preferred to do his foraging during the darkness. His tasks still unaccomplished, he glided onward.

As chief scientist for the colony, he was also collecting samples on the surface for an experiment he was conducting. Ator, his mate, would expect him back to the nest soon. He did not expect anything out of the ordinary, so he flew from surface to surface, merely going about his business.

All the while, Axreal was off duty alone at the agreed upon interval. She sat centered in her meager habitat podule; the plastic abode was a miniature technological biosphere. She had made sure that everything was in order. She sat still, with her legs folded, placing herself in the middle of the main compartment. Next, she initiated one of her seizures. It began. A hundred thousand vibrations. Axreal blurred into the background, leaving behind an afterimage. A ghost. Vanishment. The Breach.

Simultaneously, Jerish was off duty. He stood alone at the agreed upon interval and initiated one of his tantrums. It began. He spun in place with a hundred thousand revolutions. Jerish blurred into the background like an afterimage. A ghost. Vanishment. A successful breach.

Axreal and Jerish reconnected and met up to explore again. They hoped they would find what they needed to be able to survive outside. They could then break free from their prison permanently. Only this time something was terribly wrong.

"Jerish you don't look right," Axreal said.

Jerish turned away from her so she could not look him straight in the face. "It's nothing really, I'm ready to go."

"No, wait a minute, I hear something strange," Axreal demanded with concern. She noticed bruising all along the right side of Jerish's face, "It's coming from you. Move your hand out of the way. Let me see what's wrong. WHAT did they do to you?"

Jerish resisted, "It's no worse than what they did to you. Let's get going!"

Axreal yanked Jerish's hand away from his face. She gasped in shock. "What in all torment is that?"

Jerish was distressed. "I don't know. It was on my face when I woke up."

Axreal questioned, "Does it hurt?"

"I am trying not to focus on it, because," he paused, "it hurts so bad I want to tear it off!"

"What is it for and why is it on your face?" Axreal said, "It's under your skin and there are lights and sounds coming from it." Shedding tears of pain and anguish, Jerish went into a raging fit. "You have to calm down," Axreal said. "Let's figure out what it is. Okay, obviously, I don't have one, so why is it only on you? It's making noise as if it's sending a signal; it's tracking your location now! What made The System suspicious of you? What did you do different? You took something back to your podule didn't you?"

"Yeah I kept a souvenir. Why should that matter?"

"What did you do with it, where is it now?"

Jerish dug his hands into his pockets. With a dumbfounded look on his face he responded, "I don't know, it isn't here, you don't think . . ."

Axreal blurted, "That has to be it, The System found it."

"I don't see how," he said.

"If it got alerted then we could be in serious danger," she said fearfully. "You especially. How can we remove it, unless we cut . . .? You might just have to bare it for awhile till I can figure something out." She could not withstand seeing Jerish in pain, but was at a loss for what to do for him.

"The System will come looking for me, and it's all going to be over. We will never see this or each other again." Jerish, resolved to try to block the pain and discomfort from his mind, but he could not help but continue to act jittery, he had the equivalent of Setiacotion goose bumps.

"Let's see what happens first," she replied. "Maybe I'm wrong, maybe it's something else. Maybe we can hide you. We will figure something out."

"I hope so."

They kept onward. They decided all they could do for now was to face things as they came. They surveyed the land ahead of them.

On their previous breaks from prison, they had had wonder and excitement to look forward to, except for the trouble this occasion. The hiking gave them the exercise they needed, which began to strengthen their muscles. The new sights, smells, and sounds stimulated their minds and exhilarated them. They benefited from these newfound sources of nourishment. It led Axreal and Jerish alike to ponder their overall experiences.

"Something is happening to us Jerish, why are we the only ones able to do this? It's as if we have been chosen for something," Axreal changed the subject and matched her stride to that of Jerish's. The long planetary night was finally approaching dawn. She knew what would further take his mind off the pain. "Have you heard those songs again?"

"No, you sound like you don't believe me."

"It's not that, I was just cur . . ." At that moment, something glowing greenish yellow flew out at Axreal. It adhered to her back for a moment. "The System found us! Get it off of me! What is it? Oh disgusting!"

The life form was accustomed to gaining its main nourishment from licking the surfaces of the land, rocks and the like for Evallious Navatilum, an appetizing delightful meal and largely visible fungus, an occasional lichen might make for a good snack. Axreal and Jerish had not noticed the Evallious fungus before and had been unable to distinguish it from the molten rock formations. The life form hastily leapt over the rock surfaces, searching for food. It had inadvertently landed on Axreal.

"It is some sort of creature," replied Jerish. He was surprised; he did not know if it was a friend or foe. Partially relieved, he said, "The System didn't send this!"

"Well it has no business on me!" Axreal blurted out as her body fidgeted and her hands flew about frantically. She felt the creature's cold gelatinous anemone like tentacles sticking to her neck.

Calm down, I'm trying to help you. I can't get it off your neck if you can't stand still." Jerish reached to pull it from Axreal, and tried to coax it off, saying, "Come here, boy."

It then slid off bouncing away. It had left a temporary impression on her neck. Axreal rubbed her left hand over the area.

"Are you all right? Did it hurt you?" Jerish asked.

"I seem to be okay. Just scared, with all that has been happening to us," she replied.

Jerish bent low to the ground to see where the creature had gone.

"How do you know it was a boy?" asked Axreal as she watched Jerish in a frenzy trying to locate it.

"Well I don't exactly know, but it seems like one."

"It attacked me, so I am not the least bit interested in coming across it again. It is probably long gone by now."

"Well I am curious about it Axreal, even if you're not. We haven't seen anything alive out here, now we know there is, and it is small, kinda cute, and different," Jerish's grayish blue eyes caught sight of the creature huddled under what appeared to be a plank. Jerish pressed his fingers to pry it loose. "It sure does feel mushy, kind of like Nedlix Gel," a component frequently used in one of The System's manufacturing processes. The gel creature let out a tiny squeak.

"Well that's it Jerish. See, it doesn't seem to want to be bothered. It isn't right to take it against its will. Please let it be," she remarked.

The sky had started to lighten up somewhat, and the dark purplish rocks had noticeable flickers of different colors to them now. The temperature warmed, and little wisps of steam rose, making gurgling sounds as they pushed water droplets up through the pores of the rocks.

Jerish cooperated and left the life form alone, and then he and Axreal turned to proceed hand in hand.

Torbot came out, much more clearly visible. He had hundreds of sticky arms that could protrude or retract fluid like into his round body, two large silky eyes, a tiny mouth, and protector pads. He stared up at the two unknowns as if appearing to say: *Do not leave me*. His inquisitive, scientific curiosity caused him to want to find out more. He thought he went unnoticed because he followed a few yards behind.

Jerish glanced slowly back. He noticed the gel creature following and whispered to Axreal, "Look, don't alert him or make a sudden move, he has come out."

Jerish turned slowly around and gradually lowered himself to be level with the life form.

"I won't hurt you," Jerish said gently.

The creature stood out in great contrast from the molten rocks and dusty soil in this region. It had an inner glow and was round in shape when it retracted its numerous stretchy gel arms. Jerish extended his palm. As the gel creature, all of perhaps ten inches across, moved closer, it reached a point where Jerish grabbed for it. As he pulled, it was only one arm he managed to tug. The cute creature remained on the ground at some distance back. On a satisfied filling of fungus, the life form weighed a little more than usual and it held its own ground against Jerish's grasp.

"Let go of it and let's see if it will follow along better, Jerish." said Axreal. "I don't want to force him. It just doesn't seem right."

The life form was as curious about them as they were of him. He was content to observe them.

"I think I will call him Torbot," Jerish announced.

"Where did you come up with a name like that?" Axreal asked.

"I haven't a clue, guess it just popped into my head," Jerish replied. He had not known that Torbot was in fact the gel creature's name and that the creature had planted it inside of Jerish's mind.

As morning continued to slowly break, the air filled with a mist. Glints of tiny prisms floated into view. The rainbow like zephyrs were a property indicative of the presence of one of Eclipsia's extremely rare unadulterated waters. Torbot jumped ahead of Jerish's and Axreal's hand-clasped stride, making a tiny splash in a puddle.

"It's as if he is now leading the way," remarked Axreal who was not always very trusting.

Torbot proceeded to direct them between a vale. Liquid never before seen by Jerish and Axreal streamed between the vale's walls. Periodically, they came across a fossil, often in areas that looked as if they had been blazed over, with undulating gouges dug into trails. Along their explorations, they encountered varying colors of soil, mud, and molten rock and boulders. Some areas looked as if the ground had been burned, others appeared contorted, trapped in radioactivity, and still other portions appeared in a more natural state. Obviously, tools of some sort had reshaped the land. There were pitted areas in which it appeared that some sort of extractions had been made; other areas had obviously been tunneled or burrowed.

Jerish turned to Axreal, "I am still afraid of being tracked. I could be endangering you and Torbot still. Maybe you'd be safer without me."

Axreal, while transfixed on the way Jerish's hair flowed and the liveliness he recently started to convey said, "We haven't seen any sign of The System showing up here. We should remain alert. Don't do anything foolish. For your information, I have no intention of leaving you stranded here. We have to consider that maybe it's not possible for you to return now. I just don't know yet. Let's just continue on for now."

Follow, Torbot planted the message into each of his fellow sojourners minds. After many miles, he announced, *Home.* They crossed over a hill and below them, a village rose. Torbot's colony housed many of his kind, the largest population thus far. Having survived the original Lam Waron invasion undetected, they made small strides in the shadows. Unencumbered, his people had gone on to build a tiny civilization, unique in all the worlds.

The Lam Warons found Torbot's people simply too insignificant to bother with in the beginning, and they had not expected them to survive. Despite the horrific ravages to Eclipsia, they had significantly evolved. Being flexible in many ways helped them survive the changes to the environment. They made advances in culture, and the sciences. With some of the village underground, and because of Eclipsia's immense size, Torbot's people went on evolving undetected for many generations.

Torbot began to impart at great length, *Understand. Each generation of my people, take the knowledge of our ancestors as valuable truth.*

Jerish and Axreal looked at each other with amazement at the extent to which Torbot could impart his thoughts.

Torbot continued, *Without having to relearn everything over again, without having to relive past mistakes, we are well suited to improve upon our knowledge and advance our people. Continued life depends on compassion and caring for each other. We need each other to survive.*

What we are taught is for our highest good. When the circumstances change, our scientists, like myself, study the situation, and make a determination in the interest of all past, present, and future concerned. Hence, we try to pass on only factual information to our descendents. We don't tell myths, and we try to live in reality. War solves nothing and we have remained a completely peaceful people. War is a failure. We know of what once befell the three species. So as not to become vulnerable, we developed a civilization based on self-reliance, hard work, and honesty. We strive to have authentic lives.

Torbot led Axreal and Jerish to his abode, further touring his colony along the way, all the while he continued imparting to them his people's way of life. He explained, *Naturally, we build things to last and endure. Frequently having to dispose of things and constantly replacing them is not good for anyone or Eclipsia and is a waste of our time, energy, and resources. We live simply, utilizing natural, low-tech means; we have no vices or excesses. What is good in life is not necessarily what is most convenient.*

Torbot's people knew all they did would affect their progeny, so they acted with special care. They held no illusions, and faced life knowing nothing comes easy. What was worth having was worth doing for oneself and putting work behind it. There were no quick and magic fixes. They tried and succeeded at limiting distractions from their goals. Inquisitive in nature, they tried always to better themselves and expand their knowledge. No one would ever come and fix everything, making it perfect.

Torbot's people wanted and trusted no outside help. The far distant past told truths of what happens if you give up your freedoms. They knew to better yourself you took care of yourself and others. Torbot's people sought to live in harmony with each other and with what remained of their planet.

The colony was comprised of hard pottery-like buildings, decorated in varying lines and box and triangular shapes. They took pigments from the different outlying soils and rocks. Numerous openings encompassed the buildings' exteriors. It resembled a prairie dog town. The people could catapult themselves from opening to opening. They stored their collected foraged foodstuffs in communal silos. Spigots dispensed food and drink to all. Ator would be eagerly awaiting Torbot's return to the nest and to listen to him regale his journey.

Torbot stopped at what appeared to be an amphitheatre. *Rest here*, he messaged to Axreal and Jerish.

Curiosity abounded as many of the gel creatures popped their bodies through the openings to get a look. Torbot went inside and told of his expedition. He relayed to them that the male appeared to be in great agony. Torbot's people knew that Jerish's body should be able to expel the intrusion. Why it had not done so yet was strange. Perhaps their confinement somehow prevented healing. On coming out, he gave Jerish a nectar to drink which was known to speed healing.

He imparted to them again, *Relax. We are pleased that your species still exists. It was widely thought that you were trapped in the glowing oviums, that you had been turned into something else. No one has ever seen inside. No one has ever returned until now.*

Torbot motioned for Axreal and Jerish to face toward the outskirts of his village. They stood agape at the edge of The Bereavement Ravine. Overwhelmed by what they saw, Axreal and Jerish gasped.

"How did this happen?" Jerish said, breaking the silence.

Look. This is your home, Torbot replied. Then pointing skyward, *this is what the ones from beyond did.*

Outstretched before them spanned the largest view Axreal and Jerish had seen yet. Every form of landscape they had encountered lay before them, along with many they had no idea what they represented.

Torbot explained that this was a historical place, *It is perhaps where they first began to despoil the land. Many died here.*

The image that Axreal and Jerish had seen of Eclipsia elicited sadness deep within them; perhaps it summoned an inborn grief. They knew what horror looked like; they existed within its walls every toiling day. This, however, went beyond anything they had ever witnessed before. Perhaps, it became a more impactful sight, due to the way in which they were becoming rejuvenated. The swelling sensation they had each experienced before on separate occasions rose up now, in unison.

Be aware. It is difficult to look upon, Torbot continued implanting the thought ideas into their minds. *The scope of what they did here is immeasurable, and it effected past, present, and future.* He hung low and bowed in reverence to Eclipsia and what she had endured here.

Discards of twisted toxic material distorted even time and space. Areas that still resided in Axreal's and Jerish's frame of reference appeared the normal range of hues and appeared to have motion. Areas fixed in radioactivity had absurd coloration and appeared like three dimensional puzzle pieces which could not be penetrated. Despite consisting of land, air, or waters, all within each radioactive piece, appeared solid and motionless. Those areas existed out of phase, and the fabric of nature remained distorted there on every level. Fumes rose, so poisonous they no longer were relative to normal reality. They formed back into the radioactive puzzle pieces. Axreal, Jerish, and Torbot had difficulty making any sense out of the ground. Fires burned for ages. Parts were beyond comprehending, irrational, and if given too much thought could cause one to go insane.

Do not ever look upon this for too long. Not all is lost however. Certainly, this has been a remarkable day. You, the Setiacotions returned. You are changed, but still resemble what we were told about and you do fit with our records. I will show you something to give you hope. Cry not Axreal and Jerish. Follow. Torbot swung in his usual curious way.

Torbot lead them back to the colony to his particular residence. Many of the distortions from The Bereavement Ravine remained isolated and could no longer interact with anything from normal reality. However, the ordinary toxins lingered at dangerous levels. Torbot's people in their wisdom built the colony far enough away and with safeguards. Once returned from inside his home, Torbot brought along a carryall.

I am glad to see that you appear better, Torbot placed the thought inside Jerish. The nectar caused the tracking device to be expelled, and Jerish had crushed it with his stomps. Even his bruises began to subside.

"I get the idea we are traveling far this time," Axreal said.

Well yes, Torbot declared.

"We can't stay. The System will notice us both gone soon. It already may be coming for Jerish. We will be punished, starved, maybe even terminated," she stated.

I thought you were free of the oviums, replied Torbot.

Upon hearing that remark, Jerish recalled the numerous outings resulting in grief at having not been able to remain.

Tell. What makes you not try to stay out here and make it on your own? Torbot asked. *Why must you go back?*

Axreal confessed, "We are unsure if we can survive out here."

That put a spark inside Torbot. The quest he would lead them on became even more pressing now. *Quickly, I will show you something that will convince you to stay!*

Upon the outskirts of the colony, Torbot confidently continued leading the way as the comrades strode between what looked like an enormous rib cage. Its encompassing arches reached above to crisscross the murky heavens. Their hopes rode high in anticipation of what Torbot had in store for them. Jerish grasped hand in hand with Axreal. Having small statures did nothing to hinder them. They moved onward with increasing determination.

Talrish neared its peak in the sky. It flamed now at so great a distance that it's light penetrating through the unhealthy atmosphere shown weak, like a cloudy day. They covered a large distance. Torbot encouraged them even further onward.

"Jerish," Axreal called, trying to get his attention. She struck up a conversation with him, despite the fact her palate felt dry. "You've helped me learn so much more about myself."

"Me too," he replied. "The more we seem to get to know each other the more I learn about myself. You always look out for me, and make me pay attention to what is most important."

"You make things exciting Jerish. I think things can change, and we won't always have to labor, hurt, and be misused. Our best selves appear when we are here, out beyond. We've changed and for the better."

"I so want this to last. I never want to go back! I want to be able to be free!"

The space in Jerish's chest filled with an intensity almost to a breaking point. It almost resembled a craving, a desire. No Setiacotion since their implantation into the processing facilities by the initial Harvesters, had ever had the ability to feel so strong a desire for anything.

Axreal shared Jerish's sentiments as well. She could not have expressed them herself any better, so she remained in quiet contemplation.

In confinement, they simply moved from pain, to the less painful, if they behaved correctly. They always tried to avoid pain while always carrying out the dictates of The System. They solely wanted to avoid punishment. Pain had lessons in it when it naturally occurred, lessons towards arriving at balance, or good. But The System inflicted unnatural pains that it used toward manipulation. The System never allowed them their own wills. Perhaps today would be the day they would be able to cut their shackles.

"I'm getting hungry. It's been some time since we had any rations," said Jerish.

"Now that you mention it, it has been a long time since we had anything to eat or drink."

Just as things had gotten quiet, Torbot 'screamed', *RUN*!

With that charge, about fifty of his gel arms shot out, sprung into action, and clung to some formations to hurdle him rapidly forward.

Approaching from a good distance behind was a sort of mechanical monstrosity, which furiously bolted toward them.

None of them had a chance to say, think, or do anything else but flee. What barreled down and chased after them left them only one option. They had to flee for their lives. At first, they took off together. Then they separated, taking different directions.

Axreal purposefully ripped her fatigues in a mad hurry to free up her legs, making a skirt in which to run more freely.

At some distance away, Jerish threw his hands up onto a ledge pulling himself up to move above the scene, hoping to rise to his escape. Sweat broke out and stung in the corners of his eyes. He worried about whether the other two had made it and whether they lived or not.

Torbot attempted to find a deep hole in which to hide. Then he determined that might not be the best course of action. If the behemoth continued collapsing this much matter around him, he might be buried alive. He had seen much in the way of fresh Evallious Navatilum dart by. Someday, this could prove a fertile feeding ground in spots, but it held more than that today, it held their fates.

What sought their destruction appeared like a metallic contraption of hastily assembled system parts. Immediately upon discovering that Jerish was located outside the processing facilities, The System had it manufactured. The System then released it outside. It had been programmed to seek out the tracking device inserted into Jerish's face and to make a visual record. It's primary objective, however, was to eliminate him. The destruction of the tracking device caused the contraption, instead, to aimlessly search about for him. When it happened upon Jerish, he was accompanied by a female and some sort of creature.

It resembled a careening dinosaur, lurching forward on two massive aft legs, and two tiny arms in front for catching. It had a craning neck that swayed its control center from side to side, which provided its visual sensors with a broad scope. It had a gaping mouth, and jaws in which to shred its intended catch. Within the processing facilities, it could blend right in, but out on the Eclipsian surface it looked utterly ridiculous.

Now it hurdled over rocks, breaking them under its massive weight. Scratches marked its tail where it slammed obstacles out of its way. It jumped and leapt. When descending, its head was pulled downward by its momentum.

Torbot and his two Setiacotion friends luckily met up. The contraption reduced its speed a bit and circled, unsure as to where to go. They could occasionally see its head pop up or tail lash as it crazily charged around.

Out of breath, Axreal panted in between her words. "It has to run down–sometime–its power source will have to–give out."

"Yeah, the thing is when will that be? It seems pretty charged up now–I say we try to–destroy it," Jerish offered. He flung sweat from his thick brows.

Torbot clung up the side of a rock to face them at eye level. His carryall remained fastened about him. In just the short time, he had known them, he had observed numerous changes in them. Was it his imagination or had they grown?

We must be able to turn it off, or set a trap for it, Torbot instilled. He was grateful for his protective padding. It had been very useful during this entanglement with the contraption. He wondered why Jerish and Axreal did not have similar protection. *I would like to get this obstructive nuisance out of the way so we can continue with our purpose before us. Do you have any further suggestions Jerish?*

"Suppose we do both," Jerish said boldly. "It'll chase after us again here shortly, right? Only let's have it come after Torbot and me. We could lead it up there," he said, pointing to a cliff. "Axreal could be positioned up there and it would attempt to get at her, only it can't. While it's distracted I can run behind it and climb up its tail, climb up its back . . . maybe I can wedge something into it or sever its connections."

"That sounds like the best plan we've got. Try to smash its sensors. If you knock its sight out it won't be able to see us, let alone know where it is going. What about Torbot though, where will he be?" Axreal realized her own peril in this scheme, but it did not compare to what Jerish was proposing for himself.

"He can attach to me and help me. With his ability to cling, he can get around to the contraption's front blue lights, and bust them in." Jerish was not about to let this pile of junk stand in their way.

"It is coming straight for us!" Axreal gasped. She rushed to find her way up the cliff. "Jerish, Torbot, do well. Please don't get hurt, and come back in one piece!"

The contraption approached them with full force. With Talrish to its back, its shadow overtook Jerish and Torbot. They still had no idea what to use to smash out its eyes. Grabbing a sharp rock, Jerish hoped it would suffice.

Just as planned, the contraption drove itself into the cliff wall. Axreal had made it to the top, paying no attention to her own welfare. She knew she had to carry out her part no matter what, or Jerish and Torbot would be massacred. Its head thrust back and forth, and its gripping jaws beat like a piranha ready to shred its meal. It followed Axreal's changing positions. In no time at all, she knew what to do to distract it. She began operating her mechanical arm. By extending and retracting the arm repeatedly in a circular motion, she taunted the contraption. It remained confounded.

What desperate lengths Axreal thought The System had gone to, for it to manifest in such an absurd form. She thought to herself, while back a ways from the contraption's teeth, *whatever reason The System has for not wanting us here it's great enough that it'd create something like that to kill us.*

"I can do things on my own. Jerish and I, have the power to think for ourselves and choose to act in ways to support ourselves, we have power over our circumstances," she reassured herself while clearing out the volumes of conflicting and useless system programming. She was making room for ideas and new memories.

Below, at the cliff's base, Jerish with Torbot adhered to his shoulder, had made a run for it. The contraption embodied the negativity of The System. Its smell, like burning rubber, from its joints, and the abnormal energy it gave off, sickened Jerish. He very much looked forward to taking this contraption down. He hoped he would not have to see into its eyes though. They glowed with the same eerie flickering luminance that the factories gave off.

Making his way up the tail section proved more difficult than he had anticipated. He gripped his way up the tail surface while fighting to stay attached. When the contraption's body leveled, Jerish ran part way up its back, stopping and holding firm, when it looked up.

He next reached the control top. Torbot pulled out a tool, a device he used for excavations, from his carryall and sprung it around to Jerish's hand. Jerish grasped this in place of the rock and he gouged out the machines eyes. Splinters broke out, cracking along its sensor's surfaces. With another wallop, shards of glass-like material broke off in shatters, falling like winter icicles to the dirt and rocks below. The eerie luminance no longer took up residence and the broken shards resounded with the contraption's defeat.

Jerish started to head down to retrieve Torbot's tool when Torbot imparted, *Come, we have more important matters to attend to!*

The Barons' Agglomeration

The Resort Kanda drudges gave elaborate detailing and attention towards CreXan's retiring ceremonies. They went to equal troubles and lengths for his morning arousal. CreXan deified himself and celebrated his own magnificence; certainly no one else did. They did so *outwardly*, as their survival depended on it. The more elaborate a fuss he had them make over him the more self-important he felt. There was a direct correlation between how much pomp and pageantry he insisted upon, and the degree to which he needed to be removed from the evil he caused. The more caught up in his melodrama, the less he had to face what lay at the root of his operations. Buried in luxury and material things, showered with praise and entertainments he could soon forget reality. Just with a thousand-room floating Resort alone, its numerous vaults and vast holdings, he had plenty to explore and be distracted by.

"GET LORESE IN HERE NOW!" CreXan demanded.

A meek, short, and what could be considered elderly Kanda drudge had been posted to sleep watch. She occasionally had the unpleasant duty throughout the night to remove any moltings, without disturbing her master during his sleep, so as not to dirty his sheets. She cowardly ran to CreXan's side. So docile and beaten down, she, unlike Lorese, dared not even harbor an insubordinate or rebellious thought. She feared he could be so powerful as to be able to read her thoughts, and not even in her thoughts did she feel safe.

"You stupid fool. You stand there as a Lam Waron larva. That is why there aren't any more of them. They were weak like you and we eliminated them. If you don't want to suffer the same fate, I suggest you get Lorese in here now!"

The elderly drudge nervously complied and sped away as gracefully and as quickly as she could manage. Upon exiting, a tall Kanda doorman gave her a disconcerting look. He knew the old drudge had gotten CreXan off on a bad start and he was sure to also suffer some of the consequences. The old drudge returned with Lorese. CreXan compared the two. One of his eyes registered Lorese, and independently in the other stood Marese. The latter repulsed him.

CreXan bolted toward the elderly Kanda drudge, thinking, *Eeehhh, I have kept you long enough. You are too ugly to foul up my beautiful Haven.*

With that, he moved his large segmented body, the weight of which pressed down on her, crushing the old drudge on the hard floor. One of his three hind legs caught her up in mid-air behind him and threw her out of his view, smashing her into a pillar.

"Remove that and get it out of my sight!" CreXan ordered. He had a busy interval ahead. The itinerary had arrived and he had plans to devise. He had no time for an old drudge.

"Lorese, see to my belongings, and have them placed aboard. While I am gone, you have your orders. I also want this redecorated." He made reference to the main suite. "Everything new when I get back. Oh, and replace the taller doorman, and I want a victory celebration when I return. There will be only three other Barons left when the Wamp Agglomeration is concluded!"

"It will be done for you," she said. She was quick on the draw and wise to take his lead. Lorese continued to impress him, saying, "You are victorious, and soon to take your rightful place, none other is as great as CreXan. You have outlasted them all. We of the Haven will revel in your triumphs." She thought to herself instead: *Maybe if we are lucky you'll be the one to get sacked. I really had to pile it on thick this time. Things mustn't be completely guaranteed, as he seems to think they are. Poor Marese. She'd been faithful, a little too faithful I think. He hadn't found her appealing in cycles, I guess she outlasted her usefulness to him. At least she's in a better place now. That's for sure. For all CreXan has, he won't be able to take it with him when he finally does get done in. How long will 'it' live?*

CreXan's focus was solely on the trip. He hadn't the time nor desire to address The System. If he had, he would have found out what it had been up to. He would have discovered that The System had sent a contraption outside the processing facilities in search of a male Setiacotion. As it stood, CreXan gave instructions that he did not wish to be disturbed by The System prior to and during his trip. He would check in with The System after he got back. Any messages could certainly wait until then.

"GET ME ABOARD!" shouted CreXan.

The Remorans stood on the highest tier among the three species. The System utilized them for their keen and reliable mental abilities. They suffered similar abuses as the others, only not as frequently.

Remoran engineers had designed *The Alustria*, CreXan's private winged craft. They made it fast, luxurious, and powerful. It had the characteristic outer woven design of most Lam Waron craft, only the Remorans had made *The Alustria* streamlined with bare surfaces, and with the occasional patch of woven elements. Everything aboard responded to CreXan's verbal and sight commands. Everything responded with automation. *The Alustria* only required that CreXan name the destination and it would carry out everything needed to make sure he comfortably arrived there. A separate capsule deposited CreXan to his rendezvous.

CreXan thought about how it had all culminated to this point. Lam Warons could have long life spans if unhindered. With enough resources, could one truly live on forever? Blasting between the atmospheric bridge of The Sisters of Geridine and slowing down engines out beyond, CreXan set aside his musings as *The Alustria's* capsule perched at the Baron's Wamp Agglomeration space platform.

The platform served strictly as a secluded hiatus, where the remaining diadems met to re-avow their tenants, review profits, vote the weakest performer off, then celebrate and revel in victory. CreXan had scurried these gaudy cavities every half decade before. He thought about how many Lam Warons had passed this way and how inferior they'd all been. Each time the number of Barons had grown a little smaller. That was the good news. He would be glad when his presence would no longer be required at these meetings and he could be elsewhere.

CreXan would have to give a mesmerizing and convincing presentation, a dazzling summary of profits. If all went well, he could retain his standing as a Baron. He would have to convince the others of his supremacy, while fending off their equally aggressive determinations.

For some assurance, he held Syphexan, the youngest of the five diadems, in his grip. CreXan had arranged for his allegiance ahead of time, in exchange for his not reporting Syphexan's subversive activities. CreXan had discovered that Syphexan had been rewarding his slaves and allowing them privileges, like extra rest, food, and clothing. He had also been allowing consumer worlds to skimp out on debts and he allowed expensive materials to go concentrated full fledge into manufacturing instead of being spread thin. Syphexan agreed not to vote for CreXan, if CreXan kept this information secret.

About the other three Barons, he remained unsure how they'd vote. He would have to use a combination of seduction, blackmail, trickery, fraud and falsification to persuade them not to vote for him. Everything would then come down to how well CreXan could master these forms of manipulation, as well as how and against whom to best apply them.

The assessment of CreXan's profits, holdings, and his new

requisitions would all be factors in determining his continued standing, for only the most conniving, mongering profiteer, the greatest hoarder, ruthlessly aggressive at owning it all, could be worthy of it all. Only the most merciless could squeeze out the fullest profits, and only he would be fit to inherit all Lam Waron' holdings. To be the LAST meant you were the best, and all others fell away in inferiority. Without competition, the final Baron could, without a shred of doubt, own the entire operation and reign, without question, supreme.

CreXan retired from his long trip. He luxuriated in his accommodations, all the while the view of the stars and nearby astral bodies entertained him. His slitted eyes passed over Eclipsia. From this distance, she was but a dim speck amongst billions of entities in the Serendipity. He had not known it was her. She had given nearly all she could, and in a short matter of time, she would not even amount to a vague memory. Eclipsia was a means to an end, nothing more.

In the tyrant's absence, the Haven became quiet. No echo of CreXan remained. Lorese stole away to CreXan's personal suite and locked herself in. She released a portion of her pent up hate and went into a rage destroying everything.

"Aughhh!" She hurled the artwork across the room. "That's for Marese!" She slashed the curtains, screaming, "This is for all the Kanda you abused!" She shattered vases, platters and the like, all save for the mirrors. CreXan adored his mirrors. "This is for every time your filthy eyes looked on me!" She tore open the comforters. When her fit stopped and her body could not be called upon any more, she sat on the edge of what had been CreXan's bed and remarked, "Oh, that, felt, gooood!" Lorese thought to herself, *I've got other business to attend to. I need to get the drudges situated.* She immediately went to work, hailing the drudges into action.

"The master wants the main suites redecorated. I have already taken care of everything in there," she said, pointing to CreXan's personal suite. "All you need to do is clear it out." Lorese turned her back to them and quickly made her way down the hall.

The Kanda who were ordered to redecorate set out to choose an appropriate style and matching color scheme. Lorese sent in an urgent requisition to The System for the necessary supplies and wares.

The Kanda began throwing out the old furnishings, clearing and cleaning the rooms. Upon entering CreXan's personal room, they stood dumbfounded when they saw what Lorese had done, but their shock quickly passed as they reverted back to their ingrained programming. They followed her directions and began to pick up the mess she left behind in her rage.

In a number of intervals, an unpiloted automatic control ship, an ACS, would arrive, bringing the finished goods.

Lorese said, "The master wants an extravaganza upon his triumphant return." She began delegating a multitude of duties.

The Kanda youths responsible for the party put everything together, including magnificent speeches, newly composed musical orchestrations with newly developed instruments, elaborate entrees, and custom designed handcrafted original gifts.

Armed with her feathered sprucer, Lorese made a mad dash for CreXan's office. Once inside she safely returned her keys to her breast pocket. No one would notice what she was up to. She rummaged through his personal belongings while collecting evidence for her ever-growing record of CreXan's wrong doings, a chance she got only once in every five years. CreXan would not notice the disarray to his personal effects, as he never extended his own effort to keep them neat.

"I don't believe it. I found the evil worm's password!" Lorese jubilantly called up his floating interface. The holographic imagery descended before her. With the use of her eyes, she entered the password, and a jingle signaled her acceptance. She had some access to The System. On the interface a fluorescent pink warning nearly blinded her.

It blinked and announced unceasingly: "ESCAPEES, MISSION FAILURE, ESCAPEES, SETIACOSIAN RECOVERY UNIT NOT RESPONDING, AWAITING INPUT . . ."

"What is going on? All hell is breaking loose. What is a Setiacotion Recovery Unit?" Lorese called up for a description and a detailed diagram of the contraption appeared. It played back the Setiacotion Recovery Unit's failed mission. "There they are! It found two of them!" She zoomed in. "And what is THAT? IT'S ALIVE, it's an alien!"

The interface showed images of the escaped Setiacotions on screen. Jerish was easily identified. The System identified his companion to be Axreal by determining that this was the only Setiacotion who had this particular retractable appendage. As for the alien, The System indicated it as simply unknown.

Lorese said to herself, "Incredible. They are actually outside The System." The play back came to an abrupt end. "If they survived they will need my help. What if I input 'ignore', and delete all the pertinent files. That should at least give them some time. For The System to have no record I will need to delete all files pertaining to them, the alien, the recovery unit, and this entire event."

With that, Lorese input the command 'ignore' into the interface. Then she found and was able to delete all pertinent files. The florescent pink warning shut off and it announced: Input received. With her nerves further roused, she quickly shut and locked the office door behind her and returned to continue directing the drudges.

In the meantime, aboard the Wamp Agglomeration Platform, CreXan continued with his musings. He wondered what it would be like in a decade's time when it came down to the last two Barons. *How will I assume final possession of the Lam Waron operations? It may result in an all out fight, would meeting here even take place, the other Barons won't simply agree to go by the figures.* One thing he knew for sure was that it was going to be him and one other, *Perhaps*, he thought, *I am so clever and beautiful,* CreXan admired his reflection in one of his intricate mirrors. *I should start The System to manufacture defenses. It will have to utilize hidden resources. I need all resources to go into profits so that I can be assured my standing. I will have to go way out and beyond to reap in phenomenal profits. Any profits diverted towards preparations for any day of battling will have to go unnoticed.*

After intervals spent in the way of delights and entertainments, The Five Barons assembled in the convention coliseum. Its elaborateness exceeded that of even CreXan's Resort Haven. It once accommodated thousands in its circular bejeweled channels. Now, the Five gathered at the center most part for their next appointment together. Outside of them, the vast golden hall held only the specters of those who had come here before. Vying for final control, they hadn't come to any natural deaths. They had met their final relinquishments here. These Five met each other as the strongest of contenders, each aware of the past careers of the others and of their exploits. Each aware of the stakes, they would face each other off.

As was tradition, the Barons read boldly together the Lam Waron Tenets. The Barons observed great reverence for the tenet passages. They showed the ultimate model for conducting business and guided each of the Barons on his path to total victory and total ownership. Their competiveness sickeningly rose up in a combined boisterous accord as they chanted their anthem:

Security comes from being in control.
Unlimited profit results in an unlimited life.
Owning everything is the ultimate support measure.
Always take in more proceeds then what you sell them on.
Isolate weaknesses in others and enslave them.
Keep the consumer worlds ignorant and dependent.
Keep the manufacturing worlds working for lowest possible rations.
You can always squeeze out more profits.
Your control must last all eternity.

Everything serves to make you rich.
You are complete when you own it all, for in owning it all will assure you your everlasting life.
Reap the most wealth, power, and control.

For as far back as the Lam Warons existed, all of them strove to reach this state. Each wanting it all for themselves had led to a world that could no longer support them; they had branched out in search of still more. Until it came down to these last days, within the next decade, the perfect one would arise. It was for him that all this accumulation would ultimately benefit.

Marlaxan slithered up to take the podium. Too anxious to do her own orations, she brought along a device which played back her prerecorded speech for all the Barons to hear.

"First on the agenda, I, Marlaxan, will summarize the overall state of Lam Waron operations. Demand is high, proceeds are almost incalculable. New territories and consumer worlds have opened up and been receptive. In fifty Serendipity solar systems alone we are the sole provider of food and material goods. We have no competition. Our systems continue to run at great efficiency, providing all consumer world necessities. They cannot make anything they need for themselves, and some provide none of their own food. They are completely dependent on us for their survival now. With each purchase we grow stronger, with each purchase we are made richer. While some facilities have run their course, we will continue to expand our procurement operations. We are installing new systems, acquiring new manufacturing worlds, and finding new resources."

"However, it is wise to note that we have received indications on some consumer planets that accusations are being made regarding the nature of our operations. One accusation is that the goods we supply are made by mistreated slaves. We do not need anything that will disrupt the consumers. In an effort to squelch this before it grows out of control, we propose a campaign. It will highlight that our workers receive a complete living package. In exchange for their work, they receive full housing accommodations, complete healthcare, food, and everything they could possibly want or need. 'We take great care of our people so we can provide you with the best,' will be our slogan."

With Marlaxan's speech concluding, all five Barons cheered. This new campaign should stop any complaints before they could potentially interfere with operations. It held tight to the principle of keeping the consumers ignorant. All they knew how to do was consume, and that was all they needed to know. If they ever found out about how the Lam Warons operated their systems, that could jeopardize everything. It had already happened on one world. It could not be allowed to happen again.

Marlaxan lazily joined the others while RamsyXan took over the podium. He enjoyed owning the others full attention. He saw them merely as temporary nuisances, that once cleared out of his way, would leave *him* the last one standing. He would only have to cooperate with them for a short while longer.

RamsyXan held excessive hatred towards his fellow Barons that went beyond his need to surpass them in business. His demeanor exhibited contempt for them. He grew tired of playing games and wanted to simply be done with them and assume *his* rightful place.

The task fell on RamsyXan to expound on other newsworthy events. His speech echoed off the coliseum's golden walls. His hardened shell had grown into a unique pattern distinguishable from those of the others.

"Eeehhh," he briefly released his own squeal, "Lam Waron Universal Conglomerates has received many accolades I am proud to share with each of you. Under my supreme rulership there will be even more!"

This caused a violent uproar. The other Barons grew furious at RamsyXan's brashness and they demanded he take back his words.

"Under your rulership? You mean under my rulership!" Petrexin grew venomous and outraged and spat towards RamsyXan. His crutch nearly fell out from under him.

"Eeehhh, how dare you both!" shouted CreXan.

CreXan had always had a high level of disdain for RamsyXan. He had seen RamsyXan work his way up in the most unscrupulous of ways.

"Everyone settle down!" Marlaxan attempted to maintain order. "Now is not the time for that. RamsyXan please…continue the highlights."

They all contained their outrage, for the moment.

When the room settled down, RamsyXan continued. "As I was saying, Lam Waron Universal Conglomerates has received, for the fifth occasion, the Alpha Crucis Commonwealth's highest award for philanthropic endeavors and charitable donations. We are known in most of the consumer worlds as the largest giver of currency donations to needy and worthwhile causes. We obtained this objective by taking donations from the consumers and also by adding additional costs to their goods and collecting the proceeds. In actuality, making these donations cost us nothing. We took their money and donated some of it back to them! This bought us their continued and added support, further respectability and trust and belief in our services, and we are seen as being good for their communities as well. We have been able to hide from them the fact that we only take proceeds from them. We have created for our operations the benefits that come with having a good reputation, without us having to do anything to earn it. The consumers think they are getting added value from us when in fact they aren't. We have donated trillions and it cost us nothing. In fact, most of those proceeds made their way straight back into Lam Waron coffers."

The Barons applauded in their usual strange way. They each held up one front appendage above their head and flicked their talons rapidly about the air. How wonderful to appear as such a powerful, benevolent, and impressive organization, on the one hand. And on the other hand, they reaped in the rewards of doing everything cheap, cutthroat, and dastardly.

The room grew quiet and Petrexin presented the next speech.

"FELLOW BRETHREN, gathered are we here again for the Wamp Agglomeration, each to present record of our current accumulations. Only one Baron can someday own it all. We are here, in this the grandest of meeting places, to determine who will remain and be best suited to eventually become the supreme Baron. One amongst us today has not proven himself worthy to carry on. It is the task before us to determine who that is. In accordance with Lam Waron business tradition, the weakest performer surrenders everything, including relinquishing his life. His holdings will be divided equally between the remaining Barons. We come forth now to present," Petrexin hobbled off the podium, as it disappeared into the floor.

A circular partition closed off about the pillars of the great center. It sealed in the five Barons.

Encounter with Marshall

Marshall rested his head as comfortably as he could manage. How long his food would last he did not know. He thought about the billions of his race who had placed all trust, faith and hope, in the success of his mission. The priest had wished him luck, and had bestowed upon him the medallion he wore on his necklace, which was draped, about his chest. The religious symbols intertwined with scientific emblems, represented his world's adoption of the merger of science and religion as both having parts of the answer to the great mysteries.

What would they think if they could have seen the deplorable conditions of his camp? That environmental rover over there had cost in the billions alone, and from here, it looked like a tin foil go-cart a child could put together. No longer wanting to be confined to his craft, he set up a makeshift tent and attached it to the outside of the emergency release hatch. The craft had owned him for too long, and it remained cramped.

The nuclear generators did have an incredible life to them, so he would not be without some power. What good would that be to him if the food ran out? He had not been able to bathe regularly. He sought to keep his water reserves for drinking, so he took a washcloth bath once every two weeks, and the stench from his excrement pile started to make its way up towards the camp. Chewing on jerky stuffs kept his hunger at bay until meal times.

He knew they had done their best to supply him in every eventuality, even providing the craft with extensive shielding to make it virtually undetectable. However, in order to pursue the Lam Warons, his people acted hastily. As a result, they made a number of miscalculations. After many light years, the craft had nearly run out of fuel and subsequently drifted towards finally meeting up with the planet. When the fuel was entirely spent, he knew the craft would crash, and he did what he could to prepare for it.

I got here by the skin of my teeth. How in the hell was I supposed to ever get back? he had thought.

The air bags had inflated and cushioned the craft to some degree; they remained decompressed around the vehicle like vast white sheets of plastic wrap, the flaps of which rustled in the breeze. Marshall's body could not rise to the task of what would be involved in making such grand repairs to the ship.

Marshall touted a very sociable personality. He credited it to his admission into flight training, to meeting his past wives, to fostering a child, and to many previous successes. This mission was a direct result of those successes. He knew the price for that success would be to have to face his fear of seclusion. He was going stir crazy. In an attempt to stave off his madness, he listened to old familiar tunes. He had packed many of them for the journey. They continuously played, yet they were an inadequate replacement for the companionship he so longed for, and returning home seemed an infinitesimal possibility.

"If only they could have found it feasible to send at least one other with me! Damn their limitations! What I wouldn't do for the company of a beautiful lady right now!"

As best as he could surmise, the discolorations on his torso and his raspy breathing meant he had come down with an atmospheric disorder. After much speculation, the engineers and scientists had ventured only a best guess at what the total chemical makeup of the air would be like here. He lived according to their estimations. They had done well but not quite good enough.

The rover had proven to be another disaster. It was unable to traverse the molten rock.

He would persevere. He had survived somewhat similar circumstances in his lifetime before. This remained different because he was on his own. What other choice did he have, anyway? The least he could do he thought was to try to hold out as long as he could. He found honor in that. It was not always reaching your goal, sometimes the success was maintaining momentum towards it, he thought. He would hold fast to his goals and the people back home would have expected nothing less, even if this were all that remained of their attempt.

The long days spent in exile continued to accumulate. The storms overhead had passed. They had been somewhat caustic. "Oh, but there are nearby signs of what I was sent here to find." Marshall announced this upon seeing the familiar burrows, striations, levels of soot and discards, and the numerous dead remains about.

Well, he thought, *maybe all that comes of our last fight is that I survived long enough to try to track them down, wasn't that where we were always going? As far as our limited bodies and abilities could take us, or just beyond?*

Marshall lay down on his mattress. A foot journey would result most likely in death. The immensity of the planet made it hard to find success in that he could simply hike his way to the Haven. Just as his eyelids began to lower, he saw two figures approaching.

"Now I know I must be hallucinating." He shook his head to clear his sight of the imaginations. However, they did not go away. They got larger. "My God, no it couldn't be, those are two children! What would they possibly be doing here?" He jumped up, ignoring the stiffness and pain in his damaged knee.

At twenty, he had been very strong. Now at thirty, what he lost in physical strength was more than made up for by mental strength. This trip had taken many tolls. Was he so isolated that he had succumbed to seeing things? He had to wonder.

Once upright he attempted to get a better look, a strange ball danced around them. It appeared to have changing tethers. Packed along his suit leg he had safely tucked his sidearm. He abhorred violence. This tool served to take out a disease, nothing more. He vowed that he owned it for only that purpose. He lifted his cap, the buzz cut underneath remarkably, besides his music, was the one luxury he routinely got. He wiped away the perspiration and replaced his cap.

Marshall did not expect to encounter any higher-brain carrying life forms. Lam Warons in this stage of the planet's takeover would have all higher-brain carrying life forms incorporated into their processing facilities. He had seen the cancerous signs of them being in full production when he crashed here.

Marshall thought about the devastation wrought to his own home world. The Lam Warons had uniquely ran experiments there and had taken parts of it into servitude, they had poisoned and raped its natural environment, but they also held control over the rest of the populace by making them entirely dependent as consumers. The Lam Waron processing facilities, being the sole providers of all material goods, sold them everything and they turned over their money, and with that, they turned over their ownership, wealth, power, and control. When his people woke up to what was transpiring horribly in other parts of their world since the Lam Waron take over, they weakly attempted to oust the Lam Warons. Few in numbers the Lam Warons did temporarily retreat. Covert operations led to the discovery of other Lam Waron occupied planets.

Marshall's people sent hunters out to track down the controlling Barons. They thought it better to go on the offensive and push the Lam Warons back to at least buy themselves time. That is how Marshall ended up here. His mission was to land safely, follow instructions on how to detect a Haven signature location, and carry out plans to secretly infiltrate the Resort. From there, he was to remove the Lam Waron diseases if possible. This new location stood in the later stages and they did not expect there to be many in the way of Lam Warons. Perhaps there would only be a few, and if lucky maybe only one.

Marshall started scanning for Haven signatures when he first arrived, and he did have a basic idea of its location. How he could get there, on a bad knee, and how he could carry food to last that journey were questions he did not have the answers to.

When he thought of what had happened to his world, the millions tortured and abused in those hells, all the while the rest of the world lived ignorant and dependent on their suffering. All the while, they gave away their things of real value in exchange for "valuables". Little by little, they had given up full control of their world to the Lam Warons. Marshall knew he must not give up. If allowed to return, the Lam Warons might attack and return everyone to slavery or worse.

They did not suspect the Lam Warons would return right away, but maybe come back in some greater show of force. They left behind disaster, poverty, disease, fallen cities, fighting, chaos, misery, deformity and death. The last bastions of wealth refitted spaceships and boarded them with hunters in an attempt to go on the offensive. They had them on the run. If they pushed them far enough out, maybe they would stay gone.

Marshall limped, dragging his injured knee behind him, as he approached the figures.

"Hello there!" he waved. Marshall heard their speech. He realized they were in fact very real and he could make out some of the language of The System. The incorporated of Marshall's world, upon their release, had also come out speaking the languages of The System. Marshall realized he would be able to communicate with them.

Axreal, Jerish, and Torbot could make out the tall life form and his encampment and the rusting vehicle in the background.

Torbot advised, *Caution. I am unfamiliar with this species; it does not appear to be from our world. We should observe it from afar, make a logical assessment, and at the first sign of malicious intent or trickery, we will need to flee. We should not rule anything out, good or bad.*

Torbot contemplated what he should impart to the life form's mind in the way of a subtle hint. He only ever did so in the most ethical of ways. When sending his thoughts into the minds of others, it was always with the intention to make the encounter a mutually beneficial one, or to impart pertinent information.

He did not yet gather the life form's intentions, so he remained reserved, then instilled: *Peace, we are friendly and merely wish to be on our way.* Toward the Setiacotions he imparted, *Notice, it appears we have another obstacle before us; it is not much further to our destination, I promise. Let us be very careful, as this could be a trap.*

"Torbot, I'm worried what The System will do next," said Axreal.

That is why we must proceed with caution.

"It's okay, I am peaceful," Marshall said. "I am not here to cause you any harm."

Marshall tried to bend lower to get to eye-level with the children; the two appeared to allow his approach. The closer he got to the children, the more their differences became apparent. They looked so much like they could be his child yet their skin tones, odd shaped ears, and toiled, wearied look, among other things, defined them as aliens. He was unsettled, yet was grateful for some sort of interaction. The tethered ball moved and blinked about, revealing itself to be alive.

Jerish stepped closer, "Who are you?"

JERISH, not so quickly.

"It is okay, I promise I will not harm you. I am a hunter, you could say, but that is only one aspect of me."

"Well what are you hunting for?" wondered Jerish.

"I was sent here to Eclipsia on a mission to eliminate the Lam Waron."

Torbot noticed the creature's injury. If he was in fact who he declared himself to be, it seemed that the creature had a restricted ability to move, and appeared to have trouble breathing. Torbot still felt apprehension. It was told that the ones from beyond used all kinds of fabrications; this could be one of them in disguise to lure Jerish and Axreal back to the oviums. Torbot chose to continue to observe, he knew he would have the best chance for escape if necessary, and he then might be able to assist them.

"What are the Lam Waron?" asked Jerish.

"They are the ones who use the processing facilities, and most likely have your people enslaved in them. They tried to possess my world also,"

Marshall explained.

He refers to the ones from beyond. Torbot imparted and clarified to Axreal and Jerish.

Jerish never had reason before to believe that it could be something living that was behind The System. Axreal also felt astounded. The System had always been just that. It had been the final authority in everything. Now it seemed even more complicated. These Lam Waron had never shown themselves, the Remoran instructions in the nurseries never made mention of them. How odd, they both thought.

"How did you get hurt?" Axreal asked.

"It is a long story. Perhaps we can go back to my camp. I can get off my leg and if we sit for awhile I can tell you all about it. You seem tired and could maybe use some rest."

Wait, Torbot instilled to the group, then alone to Axreal and Jerish he imparted: *We have a mission of our own; we do not need any further diversions. This could be a trick still.*

Startled, Marshall responded, "Did I just hear that, in my mind?"

"Yes," Axreal spoke, "That is how Torbot communicates."

"You mean to tell me the ball plants thoughts into our minds?"

"Exactly," said Axreal.

"Wow, that is really incredible."

Torbot took offense at Marshall's 'ball' remark and shifted his silky eyes looking side to side.

"Look," Jerish pointed, "I don't think he likes being referred to as a ball. By the way, what is your name?"

I advise caution, we should have examined the creature from a distance first before approaching it and we really need to get back on track and move on.

"My name is Marshall. I'd be very interested to know what you are doing out here also?"

"Your knee is bleeding and in bad shape. It looks like that hurts very bad," Axreal noticed.

"I would like to hear more about the Lam Warons," Jerish said. He felt drawn to listen to Marshall. "I would like to find out why they have done this to our world and why they did this to our species."

"Like I said, it is an involved story," Marshall replied.

"Maybe it is worth hearing," Axreal said, trying to convince Torbot. *Tell, how do we know you are truly who you say you are?*

Marshall reached into his pant leg. Torbot fervently imparted, *Danger. It has a weapon, get down!*

"This is my protection," Marshall threw his sidearm out amongst the rocks. "Now I am defenseless, I don't know how else to show you, but I am speaking the truth."

Torbot studied the situation. It would sure be an elaborate Lam Waron ruse, and the details in the background did help to substantiate Marshall's claims. After Marshall appeared to hurl his weapon, Torbot, Jerish and Axreal apprehensively rose from where they had dropped and looked up.

Marshall held his hands up above his head. "Please, I am alone. I haven't seen anyone. I am not well. I'm tired, lonely, and hungry. I really can't do anything to harm you!"

"I think we should give him a chance and trust him," remarked Jerish. "He seems honest."

Very well, you two can further approach and I will remain behind as a safety precaution. We will still have a way then to get out of this if it somehow turns bad.

Jerish turned toward Marshall. "I call myself Jerish. This is Axreal, and our pal is called Torbot."

Torbot leapt, taking notice of a disgusting smell. He rolled his eyes and squeezed them tight. It appeared to be coming from the life form's droppings.

Jerish, with Axreal closely following, stepped up into the encampment. Axreal turned to give a glance back at Torbot. The look on her face expressed that she hoped they were doing the right thing.

"Fine, let's sit under the tent," Marshall said. He motioned for them to make themselves comfortable. They positioned themselves on the weathered mattress. Jerish sat closest to Marshall. "You know, I have a son...had a son Kurt, about your height, Jerish." Marshall could not vouch for the Setiacotions ages. "He was a lot like you though." Marshall held Jerish's shoulder, noticing an unusual difference in Jerish's body temperature. Marshall thought to himself, *You'd probably be more like Kurt if not for the horrible things which have been done to you.*

"Where is Kurt?" Jerish asked.

"Well, I left him back home with his mother. While I attended flight training, she chose another life and we parted. I remarried shortly thereafter. My last wife regrettably died during the Lam Waron ousting from our world."

"So, you've been here a long time?" asked Axreal.

"Yes, you can say I am stranded. The ship is inoperable, and I am way out of communication range. I crashed here on Eclipsia, far from where I was originally supposed to set down on the surface. It was during the crash that I hurt my knee."

Intriguing, the ones from beyond have been ousted from other worlds, Torbot contemplated and peered out from behind some camp equipment. He had gone around the back of the makeshift tent to get close, yet not so much as to reveal his location. Hearing their conversation mattered most.

"Yes," Marshall said. He had to get used to this new form of communication he experienced between himself and Torbot. "I hear your friend but I can't see him. Anyways, the Lam Warons have a distorted nature. They seek wealth, power, and control, and manipulate worlds to fit their purposes. They roam the universe searching for susceptible worlds rich in resources. They take them over, steal from them, and enslave the people, turning everything into giant factories. The Lam Warons sell the products to the consumer worlds and they get rich and start taking them over. Only they can never satisfy their greed. They cause strife, pain, and misery wherever they go. Eclipsia is just one of their holdings. We discovered numerous other places, too. Eclipsia appears to be in the final stages. From the looks of it, she has given everything she has. I don't suspect the Lam Warons could use her much longer."

"Good then they will be gone!" Jerish said, elated.

"Not so fast, Jerish. That would be a great answer, but the Lam Warons lay waste to the planets they use up. My people sent out reconnaissance missions at home. They retrieved data revealing a few closer Lam Waron occupied worlds. We sent hunters there also. Eclipsia is the farthest away, and the least-known. It seems, judging by the extensive processing facilities, to be the largest manufacturing world with the largest enslavement."

Still finding it hard to believe a life form ran The System, Jerish inquired, "What do the Lam Warons look like? I don't recall ever seeing one."

"That would be correct; they remain hidden, and have abilities to disguise themselves and what they are doing. They are very ugly inside and out!" Marshall said, giving further elaboration.

"How are you going to be able to hunt them if your knee is so bad?' Axreal questioned Marshall.

"Yeah, how are you going to hunt them?"

"Well, Jerish I don't know. I am hoping it will heal and then I can resume my search."

"Whul, is there anything we can do? Torbot might have something to give you that could help your knee," said Jerish.

Torbot came out from behind the camp equipment and openly engaged in full conversation with the group. *Well, I don't think I have anything that would be compatible with your physiology. I regret that I cannot help in that way Marshall. Perhaps I can assist in redressing your bandages . . . wait just a minute, I will be right back.*

"How did you two escape The System?"

Axreal responded, "We aren't entirely sure how it happens, but we are able to breach. We . . ."

"I enter into a sort of passage, all sorts of conflicting thoughts race through my mind, then my body spins like you would not believe. A sort of doorway opens and I enter and then reappear. I could show you, but it is a little painful."

"No, that won't be necessary. But it sounds amazing, son."

Axreal held a bewildered look. She twirled her finger through a ringlet of hair, yanking it downward like a spring. All the while she quietly tried to understand what Marshall meant by referring to Jerish as a "son".

Torbot returned, bringing along with him the sidearm belonging to Marshall. He recovered it from where Marshall had cast it away. He handed it back to Marshall.

Understandably, you will need this if you are to be successful in your mission. My people do not believe in violence; we never engage in it nor encourage it, but if you are to face the ones from beyond, the Lam Waron as you refer to them, you will need some countermeasure. They are extremely violent; all you have to do is look around to see the results. It is in the best interest of all past, present, and future that they be returned to where they belong!

"Thank you Torbot. I agree with you!" said Marshall.

Marshall sensed that Axreal felt somewhat overshadowed by Jerish's excitement. He knew the boy probably lacked for never having had a male figure in his life. Neither of them, he supposed, had known a mother or father.

"Come here Axreal, let me have a better look at you. Why you are just a little girl under all that after all. How terribly hard both your lives must have been. The thing is you have to keep going, never give up. For one thing, you never know when something worth waiting for will show up. For another, there is goodness in being alive. Take me for example. It all looks pretty grim, right?"

Axreal and Jerish both had to nod in agreement.

"Well things have a way of moving in the direction you put your attention on. If I didn't remain optimistic, remaining hopeful, the chance to make progress might come, or success might present itself and then I might miss out on it. Tomorrow the answers may come. So always strive toward good no matter how bleak things may appear. I won't give up because who knows, tomorrow everything might work out, the answers to my problems might come." Marshall took Jerish aside. "Axreal could you please give me a moment alone with Jerish? There are some important things I wish to tell him."

"Okay." She figured she could get Jerish to divulge the details of their conversation later.

"Torbot, perhaps you and Axreal might find a peek inside my ship interesting? The hatch here is open. Step up and into the left and you will find a table. After you have a look around, bring out the portable device you find there. It gives information we will need."

Torbot and Axreal both became curious.

Obvious, Marshall wants us out of the way to tell Jerish something, we can give them a moment alone.

"Thank you, we will only take a short while," Marshall said. With Axreal and Torbot inside the craft, he spoke to Jerish. "You see, young Jerish, there are some things you might need to know, much in the way I told Kurt, things a man needs to know."

"Like what Marshall?"

"A person has to know what is best; he has to have things of value he believes in and he must stand up for them. If you don't have positive, healthy beliefs and hold to them, you can be easily misled or made to do things that don't serve your best interests."

Jerish jumped in, "That's like in the processing facilities."

"Exactly. Stand for what you believe in, support those beliefs. Others might depend on you because you represent to them those positive beliefs."

"I'm not sure I understand."

"You will. Take me, for example. The people of my world trust me. So much so, they sent me all the way out here because they know I believe in honor. They know no matter what happens I will uphold and do my best to fulfill the job they sent me here to do. Therefore, with every ounce of who I am I will continue to move in that direction, even against the odds. A man can be trusted, relied on, and thinks about others. You have Axreal to look out for. Think about others besides just yourself. The time may come when you will have to face challenges, and be strong. You may have to put aside how you feel to best serve everyone."

"I think I understand; it is not just about me."

"That is right. Sometimes you are called upon to lead or take charge. You have to be resourceful, and self reliant, and courageous. I know it is soon to thrust this upon you Jerish…"

"What is it? I can understand, tell me Marshall," Jerish did not fully grasp the meaning of some of Marshall's words, but he earnestly wanted to understand.

"Jerish, you and Axreal are most likely the only ones of your kind to be out here. The Lam Warons have your entire people in bondage. I am here to hunt them for what they did to my people in the hopes that they will never be able to return to my world. We have the same fight. It is a great burden for one such as you. I can outfit you with everything I know and have. A man sometimes has to do things he finds difficult at first in order to set things right. Jerish, you will have to fight on behalf of your people, your planet, yourself, Axreal, and Torbot. Things are not right; they are not as they were intended to be. You must help to set things right."

Jerish felt a change come over him, what Marshall said made sense. He had been given this opportunity to be out here. He wanted to make the most of it. "What must I do Marshall?"

"We can talk further about it later," Marshall said. He lifted his cap and swung it back and forth to air it out.

Jerish took notice. "I like your hair. It's interesting!"

"You think so?"

"Yeah."

"Would you like yours to look like that?"

"Could I really?" Jerish said excitedly, as he was not used to receiving anything nice.

"I think we could arrange it. Should we surprise Axreal and Torbot?"

"Sure," replied Jerish. He liked receiving Marshall's attention. Having something in common with Marshall would be great for Jerish.

Marshall reached for his grooming kit and pulled out his shaver. Lops of Jerish's thick, bark colored hair began to fall to the ground.

A swelling sensation rose up again in Jerish's consciousness and centered inside his chest. "Marshall?" the Setiacotion youth said while watching clumps of his soft brown hair fall before his eyes.

"Yes Jerish?"

"I have something strange happening inside me."

"Oh, that's just the vibration of the shaver."

"No, Marshall, right here," he pointed to his chest. "It happened one time when I got separated from Axreal. And it happened once when Torbot showed me the Bereavement Ravine. And it got stronger every time we had to reenter the breach and to go back to our podules, and even just now it was strong."

Marshall paused to give it some thought.

Jerish asked. "Am I injured?"

"I don't think so. Let me see…these situations affected you somehow?" Marshall wondered. Then while pointing to Jerish's chest he asked, "And they showed up here?"

Jerish nodded in agreement.

"Like when Axreal was gone you wanted to be able to see if she was alright. Yes? You didn't like what that change might bring? Well then you felt concern."

Jerish agreed, "Whul yeah."

"It sounds like the Bereavement Ravine was something difficult to look at and accept?"

"Yep."

"And going back into the Lam Waron processing facilities had to have been miserable, especially after getting the chance to escape. That had to have felt miserable. So all these things affected the way your life was turning out. They affected your state of being and sent a sensation deep within your center. They made a wave rise up from within you?"

"Yes exactly, how did you know? You sure are smart Marshall."

"Son, that sounds like your heart. It does that for you to take notice. It can guide you. Always pay attention to it, within time you will grow to understand it more," Marshall said. He touched Jerish's forehead. "Always pay attention to what is in here," and tapping on Jerish's heart, "As well as what is in here."

Just then, Axreal and Torbot returned with the portable device Marshall had requested. Axreal looked to see if she could gather from Jerish's countenance any indication as to what their secretive conversation had to have been about. Her long lashes blinked about as she saw Jerish's new hairstyle matching that of Marshall's.

"What have you two been up to? What happened to you?" Axreal remarked as she and Torbot surveyed his scalp. She let out a smile in admiration. "Looks neat, Jerish."

"See, Axreal likes it, too," Marshall whispered in Jerish's ear then he spoke to Axreal. "Oh good, you found the scanner, this I can use to locate the Lam Waron Haven. The Lam Warons live in huge floating mansions. These they hide far from the systems they set up, and can monitor and instruct conditions from them. The Haven remains in one place. When they leave the planet for good, they take off in them. Let me show you how this works. This device is highly sensitive and can read Lam Waron Haven signatures, like material composition, even Lam Waron biochemistry. It can point us in the direction of the Lam Warons."

Us? Torbot was uncharacteristically short on words.

Marshall said, "Yes, I will need your help if we are to be successful in ousting the Lam Warons from Eclipsia."

Axreal said, "Is it possible do that?"

"Together we have a chance."

Axreal was overwhelmed with what Marshall proposed. "How can we overcome them?"

"If we are able to infiltrate the Haven, and with this we can locate it, then we have a chance to shut off The System, and all of your people can escape."

"We did take The System on before, Axreal; remember that contraption?" said Jerish.

"Yes, but that was just one machine, not the entire system!"

Torbot imparted, *Complicated, what you propose has many risks.*

"I want them gone, what they are doing here should not be allowed to go on. I say we help Marshall," Jerish announced.

"All of us want what Marshall wants. The problem is how can we do it?" Axreal wondered.

Torbot turned to Jerish, *It appears Jerish your friend is not just suffering from an injured knee, and I sense that his breathing is not normal. This may be affecting his thoughts.*

"I believe in Marshall, and if he thinks we can do this, then I trust him," Jerish replied to Torbot. He would not let his friend down. Marshall was unwell, but he did make a lot of sense.

This is a lot you ask from two Setiacotion slave children and me.

"I know this is an immense undertaking. I know the odds are not in our favor, but what else is *this* important?" Marshall said.

Axreal gave it some deep thought, then said to all, "I suppose if we don't take this on we will be saying that the Lam Warons are right in what they are doing. We will not be putting up anything in their way. In essence we will be encouraging and agreeing to what they've done. Say we don't help Marshall and we just keep exploring? The System will eventually track us down and kill us anyway. We should do something in our defense."

Horribly, the Setiacotions of eons ago, along with the Remoran and Kanda surrendered to the Lam Warons. They surrendered everything along with everyone. If someone could have stood up to the Lam Warons and put up a defense then, then none of this may have happened.

"Now may be our chance to make a difference. We might not succeed but at least we will have tried." Jerish was adamant.

Torbot interjected, *Where I was taking Jerish and Axreal to is still extremely important. Perhaps we can go there now and then come back for you. We might be better able to do what you ask of us if we are allowed to continue.*

"That sounds acceptable. I am not going anywhere right now. I can wait till you get back." Marshall did not really expect to get well enough anytime soon to travel with them. He did not yet admit to himself or them either, the fact that he would most likely never be well enough. His best hope was to pass the torch to Jerish, and outfit him in mind, body and spirit, for the oncoming challenges. While they were gone he could prepare for what lay ahead.

Marshall called over to Jerish, "Here take this for safe keeping for now. It will alert you to the presence of any Lam Waron. Take it with you son, it will keep you safe from them until you return. And Axreal," he said, removing his necklace with the gold medallion. He placed it around her neck and said, "Young lady, may you find satisfying answers to all your questions, may you always seek the truth."

"Take care," Axreal replied.

"Take care Marshall." Jerish did not want to leave.

"You both follow Torbot. Remember what I taught you Jerish. Axreal keep looking out for each other. I'll be waiting till you get back."

Marshall had felt sadness when he watched the two alien children depart. They had been gone for an Eclipsian day now. He had enjoyed their brief company. He reflected that even on an extremely far away location such as this one, the theme of childhood still played out remarkably similar to that of home. Even as alien as Jerish and Axreal were to Marshall, they still had need of a father.

Marshall lay out on his outdoor mattress. The flaps of airbag plastic beat and rippled in the distance to the breeze. Above flew the clouds. In shape, they somewhat resembled those of his home. In motion, they were completely foreign. He regrettably had not seen much of this strange world, but he had seen the most important parts.

He turned up the music on his player to the highest volume setting of his favorite tune. His knee had caused his lower leg and foot to turn gangrene. It would not have any use now. Marshall rolled to one side wrapping himself closely in his blanket. He knew Jerish would remember all he told him and he trusted that Jerish would carry out the plan. His music blasted and overtook any nearby sounds.

Funny how one works towards things one's whole life just to have them turn out differently, thought Marshall. The images of his son Kurt and his mother Charolett played in his mind. Jessica, his second wife, appeared also. She had valiantly retrieved data from the Lam Warons, revealing the existence and whereabouts of planet Eclipsia, that there would be a Lam Waron occupation there. Her sacrifice led to this mission. Because of Jessica, Marshall's people had at least known where to go. Lastly, he saw Axreal and Jerish with their gel creature friend swinging about them.

His breathing had become pained and troubled. He could no longer maintain the pictures in his mind and he could no longer tolerate the atmosphere. Below the fabric of his shirt the illness spread.

Pain surged intensely. It would be too much for anyone to bear. Marshall's lids closed never to reopen again. In his mind he formed his last and final thought: "They'll do it . . . I know they can."

Tenders of the Vestige

The two Setiacotions had long departed Marshall's camp. When Axreal turned and looked at Jerish, she noticed a small drop of liquid falling from his right eye.

They had passed over a land bridge, a small abandoned system facility and dumping grounds. All the while Torbot tried to answer Axreal's many questions. She asked about what had happened during the Lam Waron's initial attack and what Eclipsia had been like in those days. He explained as best he could.

"Is there any hope that things can get better for Eclipsia?" she asked.

Measurably, there is always hope.

"Why are we alive?" Axreal asked of Torbot again.

Youths always had a habit of asking the big questions, He thought, then imparted his reply, *Be aware, there are many responses to that question Axreal. Most important are the answers you form for yourself.*

It helps to get many opinions. Some say the Supreme Being formed us, that we live as the Supreme One designed us. In living out your entire life then the answers become clear for you. We are meant to grow, learn, explore, love, and evolve. Clearly, we are meant for more than just for survival. It is important we make the best of the opportunity to be alive. It is important to have respect for all life.

Axreal pondered what Torbot had told her. Jerish had listened with rapt attention. Both had grown very hungry and tired. Torbot, having far greater reserves of energy, surmised that his two Setiacotion friends probably lacked energy for having been in the confinement of the oviums for their entire lives.

They eventually neared what Torbot had brought them to see. As they approached, Axreal and Jerish felt great warmth and an even stronger swelling sensation birthed within them. Jerish now knew that this was his heart and to pay special attention to it in such moments. Surrounding them on a plane they did not yet have the visual perception of, a pink aura reached out for them. As they drew closer, nervousness, positive in nature, overtook them and 'a presence' sent a tingling vibration, marking their impending connection.

Torbot implanted in their minds, *Stay calm*, he noticed that they received his messages so much more easily of late.

They felt 'a presence' growing stronger as they got closer to it. Axreal and Jerish both sensed that whatever lay ahead would change them forever. The old Axreal and Jerish would be shed and live on only in memories.

The flat distance took an unexpected drop. Looking below they saw a thin taut permeable webbing which stretched to cover over a deep quarry. Underneath, cotton-like puffs of varying sized green and grey clumps formed a living carpet. An oval entrance appeared stitched out from the webbing, and contained a steep, yet inviting passageway.

Torbot took notice of a storm starting to form overhead and he ushered them inside. They started to descend. Whistles, chirps, and swooshing formed a cacophony of sorts and rose above the tree canopy to enter the funnels of Jerish's and Axreal's ears. Jerish could have sworn he heard the astral melody chiming in between the ruckus. The path led them winding and angling down to the oasis floor. Their total field of vision encompassed a myriad of creatures, and life filled the niches. The volume reached a crescendo.

Torbot observed how well things had progressed since his last visit. His people's hard work, long sacrifice, and diligence showed continuing rewards. He remained behind Jerish and Axreal, to bear witness to the Setiacotion reintegration back into the web of life. He took a scriber from his carryall to make the necessary documentations. He wished Ator could be here to see this. Before long, all of his people would hear of the event.

Maxurous Stravous, a swooping vine, took notice and swayed in their direction to greet them. Flowering buds of Orcadian Huim opened in their direction as if they were taking in the light of Talrish. Axreal and Jerish stepped into a cloud of fluttering delicate fliers, Flyter Avionious, with their multi-sized, multi-numbered wings fluttering. Axreal's and Jerish's motions sent a ripple effect across the fliers sending them into a wave formation. Tiny eyes also rotated in their direction.

Eclipsia's surviving vegetation and animal life forms took refuge and were tended to and nurtured here by Torbot's people. In fact they owed their very existence and continued survival to the wisdom and long held compassion of Torbot's people. For millennia, without tire, they tended to Eclipsia's wounded. Here in the quarried oasis, they gently tried to keep every life form in natural balance with each other. They created a wonderful living museum, but sadly it represented only a fraction of what had once been.

Torbot sprang forward to rejoin his friends, *Attention, Attention, you must show the highest respect for everything here, this is a fragile place.* He thought to himself, *They need to realize how fortunate they are to have this second chance, a second chance to regain their inheritance, if they're not careful with the garden, they will not survive.* Torbot would have much to teach them, and they would have much to learn.

Axreal observed buildings similar to those located in Torbot's village. Only here they picked up the hues of the surrounding life forms for camouflage.

"How did this come to be?" asked Axreal as she enjoyed the warmth of this place.

Long ago we discovered a few species struggling to survive here. Much care was given to them, and we etched out these quarries further to extend the living space, and brought others here to survive as well. We helped the sickly to revive and we helped the seedlings along. It has taken thousands of years to reach this point. The plants and animals here have developed and been encouraged along to be suited to the alterations in the environment. They are improving and their future generations stand to develop even better, that is our hope. Here we returned them to dignity, the dignity they deserve. Come, it is time you were fed.

"Torbot, what is dignity?" asked Axreal.

Remember, it is allowing a being to exist as it was meant to.

Amongst the fur-like low lying grasses grew Orcadian Orangeous. Their fanning orange leaves held veins which pulsated with an even more intense orange. Their leaves encircled about bowl shaped depressions which formed their centers. The centers of Orcadian Orangeous appeared cupped out of the ground. Four round plump violet fruits nestled within. Torbot retracted his sticky gel arms and rolled down to the center, where he began to wrestle two of the fruits from their attachment to the main plant.

"What are you doing?" asked Axreal, her hair lay fallen about the sides of her head. Her ringlets gathered in bunches at the ends due to the humidity inside the quarry. "You're harming it!?"

Never, you see, JERISH, Torbot sought to make sure that Jerish also paid attention to what he was imparting. Jerish, hearing his name, turned abruptly around to face Torbot. His eyes had been fixated firmly on the fruits.

Torbot continued, *All living things are related to each other. Orcadian Orangeous gives something to the whole, in fact many things, and in return she is provided with other things she needs but can't produce or get for herself. Everyone here helps everyone else. In her sacrifice*

Orangeous provides food for you. In exchange, Setiacotions probably gave her many things, perhaps protection, seed dispersal, in short she gives you life and you help to maintain hers. Each life form has a role, a purpose to serve, being able to live out that purpose and having the freedom to do so, is also what is meant by dignity. All living things receive life through their connection to the whole. That is why you suffered, the ones from beyond stole all the Setiacotion, Remoran, and Kanda away. They polluted, raped, and devastated our world. They did not belong here. They disrupted the natural order.

Torbot held out the fruits to Jerish and Axreal. Once they grasped them, Torbot quickly began to place notations with his scriber. The same writing instrument had been his father's, and his father's before him, and he would in turn bestow it, as was tradition, to his first born offspring.

An entire existence on artificial rations had left Jerish famished. He sucked the bursting juice and swallowed the pulp in deep satisfaction. Every cell in his body felt deep satisfaction. Gushes stained his face. Axreal partook of hers much more slowly, taking in the texture, smells, taste, and savoring her first ever portion.

Jerish felt such relief afterwards that he ran into a meadow, energized, and leaping with elation. He performed a summersault much to Axreal's surprise. Axreal remained taking everything in, unaware that Jerish's frolics played in meter with the long awaited return of the astral melody. Jerish tumbled and rolled into a clearing where he landed with his back upright and legs extended out in front of him. Coming to a rest there, he began hearing the familiar chimes, but for certain this time an angelic song verse unmistakably accompanied them.

For so long have I waited, all can be as it once was. Far and beyond wondrous realities lay ahead for you. Imagine wellness. All is within your grasp, all can be as it was meant.

The song resonated off the plant leaves. It filled the quarry. And this time Jerish took it to heart. "Who are you?"

As quickly as he posed the question the song lyrics ended and the melody faded. Both Jerish and Axreal could now see the pink aura surrounding everything in the quarry. It contained a great sense of peace and carefreeness.

"Such wonderful smells, are all these things living too?" Axreal said in amazement.

Yes, and they have the same needs as you and I. Life takes many forms, in that way life can be successful. Each has unique roles to carry out which in turn benefits the whole. The membrane we passed through above filters the waters to provide safe drinking, while still allowing Talrish to give the creatures energy. Understand, these natural occurring hollows contain soils and natural vents that provide nutrients. You also require proper water, light from Talrish, and nutrients to function properly. Come, here is one species you will need to become more familiar with.

"Jerish," Axreal called to him. "Torbot has more to show us."

He ran up to her, reaching for her outstretched arm. He thought, *I don't think I'll tell Axreal about the song yet, but she would be amazed.*

"That's odd." she said.

"What is?"

"There is something going on with my mechanized arm, it isn't responding to my instructions."

"Maybe it's still got grit jammed up inside it."

"That," Axreal said, "shouldn't be the reason. It has been working normally. Torbot?"

Yes, Axreal, He had hoped her body would have rid itself of that mechanized absurdity by now, in the way Jerish was able to release the tracking insertion. *Regrettably,* Torbot thought to himself, *she has had to bring that falsity here, such an ugly reminder of how deforming the oviums must have been.*

"What are seedlings?"

Understand, he imparted simply, *some of the plant life forms reproduce yielding seeds, like these, they enter into the ground where they take root and form into new versions of their parent.*

They passed between many more unusual sights, and drew even more attention as they went. They pushed their way between some thick foliage. Torbot's sticky gel arms danced in a commotion to clear his progress. Buried in the growth, the whistles, chirps, and swooshing subsided, and Axreal thought she made out a sort of chiming tune ringing from amongst the leaves.

Thick drops of iridescent condensation plopped in a sort of rain shower before them. Upon hitting the leaves, the water splashed apart into varying colors. Many of the organisms had grown healthy here together, and had a strong ability to heal themselves. Sadly beyond the safe sanctuary of the quarries, and their connections to each other most would starve and grow sick having to fend off numerous environmental hazards alone. Luckily Torbot's people and their food supplies had been flexible and had adapted well to the changes.

Torbot climbed upward. More sticky gel arms formed to his aft to push himself upward than those pulling up in front. His silky eyes held the reflection of the wide assortment of leaves as he ascended up a trunk. *Climb.*

Jerish cupped his hands to allow Axreal to step within them. She could then reach a contouring knob and use it to pull herself up. Though her mechanized arm was not fully responding, she was able to thrust it into wedges of bark to cling to the plant form. Jerish flew up the side, rapidly clawing his way up. "Look," Jerish perched and pointed upward. Axreal's shoes dangled above his head, "What are they doing?"

Notice, they are repairing the membrane, Torbot imparted, *occasionally particularly acidic storms like the one raging above hit, and they sometimes eat away holes in the protective covering. It is a regular occupation of late. We lost quite a few plants and animals during this last storm. The acid has to quickly be contained when it does get through so it won't get dispersed throughout the quarry. It is caught in bowls and dumped well out beyond the quarries. Nor, I don't believe it'd be good for the both of you to be out during such a storm. It can make us sick but we'd have to be out in it for a very long time. Evalious Navitilium and our other food sources have cells which protect them from ingesting the poisons. So we are mostly safe.*

Directly above, a small group of Torbot's people hung upside down around tears to which they had to make urgent repairs. Some worked to mesh the fiber strands and others repatched those with varying orders of the genus Mogvotie which made up the living membrane.

A lone Flyter Avionious landed on Jerish's nose. It had holes in its wings. It had been caught in the path the acid rain managed to make when it ate through the membrane. Jerish observed it closely and could see right before his eyes, the wing segments re-growing back into normal ones.

On reaching the top, the two Setiacotions perched along the rim of the hollowed tubular plant. Torbot pointed inside. *Enter.* Torbot could not prepare them for what was to happen next. He simply knew this particular plant species had been vital to Setiacotion of old. Jerish gustily jumped, plunging within.

Axreal hesitated. "What is this? Will we be alright?"

Torbot explained, *Quickly, I can't entirely explain, all I know is you are long overdue. Axreal get yourself within, the reasons will become apparent later.*

"But Torbot . . ."

Torbot grew annoyed at Axreal's hesitation and proceeded to give her a walloping push inside.

Varying sized streaks of viridian green and rust lined within the tubular plant. Its inside was wet with dew and contained a sticky substance like sap. Jerish fell into one bulb while Axreal slid into another. The sticky film grew to submerge them and the light from above closed off in diminishing degrees. Torbot remained above making notations. Axreal and Jerish remained calm inside as the liquid congealed to harden about them. It had reached each of Axreal's and Jerish's outer protective barriers, stopping there briefly. Then it entered beyond that and merged with them. They remained encased as if in a cocoon.

Torbot climbed down the sides of the plant to observe from below. How long this process would take, he did not know. He and others of his people gathered around to watch. When something did not immediately become apparent, they took turns at watch. They knew the process was essential to the Setiacotion, but what the results would be they did not know. They eagerly waited.

Back aboard the Wamp Agglomeration Platform, each of the five remaining Lam Warons sought only to further their own agendas. They owned no thoughts pertaining to what they had lost or destroyed along the way in pursuit of those agendas. It should have been a huge distress to them that the rest of their race had met with demise. But the Lam Warons were so selfish that they took no notice.

In pursuit of selfish desires, the Lam Warons had lost any ability to have sympathy for anyone. They had cultivated greed, and they lost the ability to feel for others altogether. Sadly, they had no way to recognize the harm and disease they caused along the way. So removed from compassion, they did not regard the slaves in their processing facilities as living beings. The Barons would also have no regrets either that one amongst them here would be relinquished.

The Lam Waron operations had grown and would soon dominate all of the Serendipity. If left unrivalled or unchallenged, its ways of procuring goods would be the only way to obtain them. The consumer worlds would receive food and material things based on the torture of other species and the destruction of worlds.

The remaining Barons sought what each of the others had and to add it to their own. They did not wish to destroy any of the processing facilities in the attempt to gain possession of them. So long ago it was agreed that, rather than jeopardize the operations they would meet somewhere neutral to feud. That is how the Wamp Agglomeration Platform was established.

Being the lazy sloths that they were, they decided to go by giving accountings. Weaker performers would be eliminated. Their holdings merged with those of the others. Because Lam Waron holdings then became spread over vast regions, they located the platform centrally. Toward the end, the process of doing each other in became formalized by the ritualistic ceremony at the Wamp Agglomeration Platform.

Each of the Barons had given lengthy presentations. CreXan's had been exceedingly long, much more like a pep rally. Everyone came away from it with some disturbing knowledge, however. All of the Barons had expounded on their strengths and why they were each suited to be in final control of Lam Waron Conglomerates. Marlaxan's presentation was concluding.

"You can't dispute my figures," squealed Marlaxan. She hadn't been allowed her recording device. "Take note, production capacity is up fifty percent. Tasks per minute stand at sixty-one. The consumer worlds solely supplied by my operations average at ninety percent dependency. No one else has even come *close* to these numbers. I am certainly the best!"

"These are false claims. Those numbers are unsubstantiated. You are repulsive and have the mental capacity of a zag fly," said RamsyXan.

"I agree. It doesn't matter what percentage of dependency your solely supplied worlds are at. *You* have the fewest of them!" said Syphexan.

"No more. The presentations are over," said Petrexin.

"None of this matter anyways," said CreXan. "I pointed out earlier to you the one of us who has broken our sacred tenants. Eeehhh, it is he that should be voted for!"

"We've heard enough. It is time to vote," ordered Petrexin. "You can come to your own conclusions. Enter your choice."

The Barons each secretly made and entered their selection. From the floor below rose the revolving Verdict Wheel. It would present the result. It spun, passing repeatedly over the names of the five Barons. It finally came to a rest upon the name: Syphexan.

Syphexan felt anger and disdain at having now been chosen to be the weakest. It was not true. The others had conspired against him. They were bought, tricked or blackmailed by each other. He had been tricked by trusting, even in the slightest bit, his evil brother CreXan. That trust ultimately led to his doom.

It was for that reason the mechanized tongs gripped and restrained him. His nodules pressurized about him and nearly came to burst. He squealed in anguish. Blood oozed from his slits.

"You are liars and thieves!" Syphexan said. Maybe now he realized as his life was to be taken from him that he had wasted it. Now was too late. That realization came too late for all Lam Warons, in fact.

The one thing on which the Barons would expend energy and actually do some work towards was devouring their weakest brethren. It was the one thing that they would do for themselves. It gave them deep gratification and pleasure. And they were highly motivated to do so.

"Your purpose has been served, Syphexan. Anything more you say now has no meaning. Thank you for making me richer!" Marlaxan said.

"We are all made richer," said Petrexin.

A cylindrical cage dropped about Syphexan. Its golden sides were marred from friction as it had made this descent many, many times before. It rattled until it met the marble floor. It sealed Syphexan airtight within. Then a hideous green gas filled the chamber. It was Tee-adrine, one of the most dangerous procured gasses. Setiacotion slaves on Eclipsia used it in a number of their programmed processes. Now it would render Syphexan liquefied.

Once the Tee-adrine cleared out of the cage, the four prevailing diadems inserted their drinking implements through the cage's housings. Marlaxan, Petrexin, RamsyXan and most of all, CreXan, ravenously sucked through their straws with all of their might. Each wanted to get the most. Like a thick smoothie, they savored every last drop of what had once been Syphexan. The process of devouring him would take a duration equivalent to an entire Eclipsian day. Once gorged, they would continue on with closing ceremonies.

CreXan snuggled up in the lavish accommodations of his capsule. He had most assuredly gained weight on this trip. The capsule shot out from the Platform, leaving blackened blast marks behind, and merged with *The Alustria.*

The Alustria had no apparent cockpit or flight deck, it merely took orders from CreXan and went where he directed it. While aboard, CreXan screeched out an order, "TAKE ME TO ECLIPSIA!"

Its engines roared with an equally thunderous response. CreXan was returning back to the Resort Haven.

CreXan felt some relief that he had pulled it all together for another Wamp Agglomeration. He had no regrets over the relinquishment of Syphexan; all was fair in Lam Waron business. He had to admit he missed Lorese. She had an edge, but she always knew the right things to say.

CreXan's anticipation grew large for what might be prepared for him. What surprises would be waiting at his return celebration? How would they have refurnished his suite and what gifts would they have for him?

Once back home, CreXan approached the festivities. The Kanda drudges put on the finishing touches and the orchestra began to play. They laid a hand crafted embroidered carpet before him, which depicted the Serendipity. As he stepped down on it gleefully, the drudges began to applaud. Clad in red and brown, they moved in formation and the red drudges spelled out 'Congratulations, all hail CreXan'. Then confetti began to rise and fall and shimmer all around him. Dancers also performed before him. He was brought food and drink. Then the circus from Arkeal Three performed high jinks acrobatics, animal antics, and knife juggling. The lights dimmed. When they were brought back, all had been changed and a consumer world renowned performer sang.

After the frivolity subsided, Vorsh, an invited dignitary and old friend of CreXan's from the consumer world Dimatia, took the podium. Vorsh had been treated to the festivities and been presented with a generous gift himself. He then gave a brief speech honoring CreXan. The speech praised and thanked CreXan for helping to supply his world with more affordable goods, and for raising the standard of living for all Dimatians.

CreXan's own physical form appeared to the dignitary to be similar to that of his own. CreXan knew most aliens could not withstand how beautiful Lam Warons were physically, so whenever in their presence, as a service to them, he would create an illusion about him that they could more readily accept.

As he gave his speech the dignitary noticed how happy and well off everyone appeared to be and how well liked CreXan was. They appeared to adore and worship him.

CreXan thanked Vorsh for his kind and flattering words. He so rarely had visitors. *How nice to have some on this grand occasion.*

Vorsh made his personal farewells known directly to CreXan., "It was an honor!"

Then Vorsh departed, along with the performer, to the government ship that was provided by the Lam Warons to ferry him home. For a second, it crossed Vorsh's mind, *I've never actually seen inside the production facilities. Oh well, maybe next time.* He would take word back to the elite on Dimatia. *Things are certainly great on Eclipsia! It is amazing how they produce everything for us and take such good care of our every need.*

Next would be the presentation of gifts. As was traditional for such an occasion, the drudges brought forth CreXan's handmade gifts and unveiled them before him. His first gift was a life size replica of himself. When it was unveiled, he stood erect next to it posing for his picture. His next gifts included vats of perfumes, liniments, and snack foods. Then they gave him boxes of jewelry with precious gems from the farthest away sources.

A blindfold was gently wrapped about CreXan's eyes. The Kanda doormen stood to open the doors to CreXan's suite to unveil the refurnishing. With the doors parted and with his ceremonial entourage, including Lorese, off to his sides, CreXan arched his upper torso as erect as he could pose it.

"For you Great CreXan," the drudges sang. "We present you with wonderful new luxurious accommodations."

CreXan had a hard time waiting for the Kanda to remove the blindfold, they took far too long, and he almost would have to do it himself!

Immediately upon its removal, CreXan blasted, "THIS IS NOT ACCEPTABLE!" He was not sure himself, even, if he had given the suite much of an eyeing over. He knew ahead of time nothing they could do, should ever be considered good enough. "LEST YOU ALL FORGET, I

CREXAN, Will be in final possession of everything, including the Serendipity. Do you honestly think this is sufficient–eeeeeeeeeee–for the Perfect One?" He did have to admit, but only to himself, that some of this did actually look good.

Lorese speech slurred, her mind was elsewhere and she let her voice slip out, speaking the words in a mundane tired fashion, "O Great and Wonderful CreXan…"

"Shut up, you don't have it right!" Then under his breath he said, "Incompetent." *Don't worry I'll keep you*, he continued thinking to himself. *You are apparently the best they can do, for now it seems*. He eyed over her sensuous lankiness.

She was jolted from her stupor, and she knew she had made a grave mistake. *I am never supposed to let him catch on to what I am really feeling. Damn it Lorese get yourself together!*

"WELL TRY AGAIN!" CreXan demanded Lorese's improved reply.

"Your Majesty…" She thought instead, *Incompetent? I got the job done alright; too bad you weren't here to see it!*

"Now that has a nice ring to it." *Even coming from an imbecile, you sure are dumb, but you do have a way about you*, he thought.

"Your Magnificence, all honor and glory is yours," Lorese said. She had instructed the assembly, at this point, to lower their heads to be in line with their waists and to walk heads lowered backwards. They performed this display so that CreXan could view his refurbished suite without distractions.

His eyes looked about; the rich paisley-like designs in extravagant colors did help to entertain him. He moved forward. Still hungry, he pulled off a nodule to taste. He caught what he thought was his splendorous reflection in a side mirror and he moved up closer to get an even better look. The glass was overlaid with silver molded patterns, like a narrow designed framework that extended, covering the mirror's surface. From between he could admire himself.

"What is that," he whispered inquiringly to himself, "a scratch? Lorese dear."

"Yes, soon to be leader of all." *Really the biggest thief of all.*

"What is that?" CreXan thought to himself, *did she think I wouldn't notice?*

"Where, O Great CreXan?"

"RIGHT HERE YOU BLUNDERING REJECT!" One of his appendages held her neck so that her eyeball got pressed into the glass, "Tell the drudges to get out, can you do that right? We have something to discuss."

"Everyone depart. The master wishes to speak only to me."

Once alone, CreXan addressed her. "Now, Lorese, what went on here? Should I have other concerns?"

She thought, *For goodness sake it is only a scratch.* Then she responded, "I am extremely sorry Your Gracefulness. I will requisition The System immediately to have this replaced. I take full responsibility for spoiling your image." But instead she thought, *Yes you should be concerned. This planet, it's polluted and it is about to collapse, and what of the lives you've destroyed? I can't take this much longer!*

"That is not what I asked you!"

He hoped his new drudges, on the new world, would better expedite his wishes.

"I don't, Your Grace, know what you mean."

"I have other ways of finding out what went on here. I would like to hear it from you…never mind," CreXan scurried out the suite's doors and turned to the stationed doorman. "Keep her here. Under no circumstances is she to be let out."

That had been clearly too much work, so CreXan decided to relax before proceeding with his investigation. "Bring forth my dinner and entertainment!"

CreXan slid aboard the Resort skid. He used this for his long distance trips inside the Resort. He ordered it to take him to the dining chambers. One chamber down the hall the Kanda had prepared a feast, a short play, and for dessert Citmop. After gorging, he reminisced about the devouring ritual. Syphexan had tasted good. He would have to have the chefs whip up something just like that so he could taste it again. He did not want to wait five more years for the *taste* of victory.

With dinner completed CreXan had the skid stop off at his office. He had the interface descend about him. He entered his password. He eyed and clicked it to open a visual record of his suite during the duration for which he attended the Baron's Wamp Agglomeration.

"That freaky Kanda drudge, she's headed for the heap!" He ordered The System to have a replacement for Lorese sent immediately. "System, play a visual record for my office during the same period. Eeeeeehhhh,

Lorese meddled with the interface. Zoom into this area and magnify."

CreXan could not believe his slitted eyes. He watched a recorded image of the interface showing a video of a male and female Setiacotion running, obviously out on the surface! And a creature appeared along with them!

CreXan shouted, "That's not possible, it can't be, yet there they are! How did they do it?" CreXan then asked The System, "Where are the escaped Setiacotions now?"

It responded, "There are no escapees. All current slaves are accounted for."

How can that be, CreXan thought, "I just saw you playback a recording of two Setiacotions and an 'alien' fleeing from a contraption you devised to apprehend them! Continue playing the recording of my office!"

CreXan watched as the visual of the Setiacotions abruptly ended. CreXan watched next how Lorese had deleted all the files pertaining to Axreal, Jerish, the unidentified creature, and all files related to the Setiacotion Recovery unit.

"Restore all deleted files," he commanded.

"Restoration complete," it noted.

CreXan grew concerned, "Why was I not notified that a recovery unit had been manufactured?"

The voice of The System announced, "Orders were received and implemented. No disruptions or communications were to be sent to you. All messages were to be held for you until you returned to access the interface."

"Damn, that's right!" CreXan fumed. "System, how did they get out from the impenetrable barrier of the repelling wall?"

The System searched. Then it announced its findings: "No security breaches have been made to the repelling wall. No variations or fluctuations in its energy field detected. Could not be accomplished physically. Other means indicated."

CreXan had heard all he needed to. He eyed and clicked urgent commands into The System. A redistributor ship latched onto the massive Resort Haven and lifted it upwards, creating a wake across the acid sea. The Resort Haven vibrated, its great weight straining the redistributor's engines. It took CreXan and his Kanda slaves into orbit around Eclipsia.

Below on Eclipsia's surface, the processing facilities had eaten her away. The Kanda had no idea that they floated hundreds of miles above Eclipsia. CreXan could still command The System from above with equal callousness.

"I have to be safe up here," he squealed, while trying to reassure himself. He needed a way to catch the escapees. "I won't let two malformations disrupt me or my operations!"

He boarded the skid and returned to his suite. Lorese rose quickly, not wanting him to see that she had been sitting on his new bed. "Lorese, it seems I was a little harsh earlier with you. It is after all a minor scratch."

That seemed odd to Lorese, *CreXan never allows any opportunity to punish go by.*

"Lorese, you have had a busy set of intervals, with the refurbishing and celebrations and all, you need some time to yourself. I will direct the drudges to prepare my retiring. Relax in your quarters."

"Thank you, O splendid CreXan." *What is the devil up to?* she wondered.

Lorese might soon get her one small wish. She would not see the maggot's slitted eyes and nasty body for several intervals. Back in her quarters, she awaited her return to duty—and her rations that seemed very slow in coming.

After several watchful intervals and with repairs to the membrane successfully completed once again, anticipation rose high among the quarry's gel creatures. All of them gathered about, their silky eyes staring ahead. A few days before, a container of sorts—much like a giant walnut—had fallen to the oasis floor. It had formed from a bulge that had emerged on the outside of the tubular. It had grown hard and podlike. Once dried, it broke off. It was about one-and-a-half times the height of Jerish. A split had formed down the center and started to spread. How would Axreal and Jerish emerge?

Torbot felt wonderment and thought to himself how extravagant life had to have once been on Eclipsia, what abundance there must have been, what incredible life forms might have existed but now were lost for all eternity. Their special unique gifts, contributions, and possible abilities lost to the past, present, and future. If the Setiacotion were any example, life on Eclipsia must have once been phenomenal. The entire world must have been one great garden.

The sides of the container split into four shells which quickly fell away. They rolled back and forth on their curves until coming to a rest. Like a released vapor, a pink aura flew out. Standing tall within, Axreal and Jerish had undergone a metamorphosis. Two taller, vibrant semblances stood in their place. Signs of the harsh factory life had been completely stripped away. They now appeared to be in a full radiance and had transformed into youthful adults. Both had gained new size, abilities, and dimension.

Torbot could not believe what he saw. Nothing could have prepared him for this.

Axreal's hair fell more closely and gracefully to her sides, her ringlets in ever tighter curls, her nose slightly more refined, her features gained an air of wisdom. Gone were her burned-in scarifications. She now appeared a young woman.

Her artificial arm had separated. It lay on the ground, malfunctioning in a yellow green goop. In a miniature scuffle between nature and machine, the goop raged on with the arm. The goop appeared to be breaking down the arm's metals. The machine jerked and twitched about. Nature seemed to be winning.

Jerish also acquired a more mature appearance; his body, like Axreal's, gained in form, musculature, height, and tone. He, too, no longer had the burned-in brands that marked him "owned" as a system slave. His appearance commanded respect—he had an air of confidence about him. He appeared a young man.

Jerish spoke first. His voice had deepened, with only a hint of the prior

Jerish within it. He tucked his hands into his armpits, then lowered them along each side of his torso. When his hands were fully extended past waist level, he turned his palms forward and spread his fingers apart asking, "Whul, what do you think?"

As if on stage, both Jerish and Axreal stood before the applause of the gel creatures. They could not contain their excitement and awe; Jerish and Axreal heard the entirety imparting ecstatically towards everyone, themselves included. This caused an uproar, and Jerish's and Axreal's minds were filled with the gel creatures' unified jubilance. The gel creatures sent out word that Axreal and Jerish would need new attire, and other gel creatures responded by creating appealing garments for them out of recycled clothes.

Many of the quarry's life forms turned in attention towards the event. The gathering vines of Maxurous Stravous and the flowering Huim buds opened, receiving and taking in the positive energies that centered on two matured Setiacotion.

Jerish kept his gaze looking forward to embrace all those drawn about him and Axreal. He reached down to grasp Axreal's right arm as they proceeded to step out from between the fallen shells of their encasement. He acted surprised when he touched her arm and did not feel metal. He gripped her tighter, signaling that he was aware of what had transpired. Axreal now had two normal arms!

Axreal turned to look at Jerish. She had grown to appreciate Jerish's attractiveness. Now she could more ably appreciate him, and she thought how even more remarkable he appeared. Both Axreal and Jerish understood and felt the changes that had taken place while encased within the tubular.

Torbot, referring to Jerish's and Axreal's recent events, imparted, *Marvelous! That should convince you both that you can do more than just survive out here!*

Axreal spoke. "Yes, dear Torbot, it all makes sense. This is where we belong. We never were meant for that existence."

Jerish responded, "Torbot my friend, thank you and for what your people have done here. We are never going back! We are free!"

Their minds, bodies, spirits, and especially their hearts told them so. They were free!

Torbot imparted, *Magnificent. You have both been returned to dignity. Now it is time to do that for all.*

Catastrophe

Torbot, along with the newly matured versions of Axreal and Jerish, set out from the quarries to return to surprise Marshall. He would be astonished to see his two friends after having under gone the metamorphosis. After a short hike, they stood captivated at what loomed miles above them. High above the colorful airs, a trail of bright smoke rocketed across the sky. A deafening blast boomed and rumbled with megaton force. It was the trail of a vacuum ship as it readied to burst through the atmosphere. Its destination, Urxis Minor.

"Don't those look like dozens of habitat podules embedded on its surface?" Axreal asked Jerish.

"They are," Jerish replied.

Explain, what are habitat podules? imparted Torbot.

"You don't want to know," Jerish and Axreal spoke together.

"What a crazy sight that is. Where do you suppose they are going?"

Axreal wondered.

Moments later, torpedoes bombarded the craft. It exploded, and burst into a fireball. Many of the podules ejected. They appeared to get larger and larger as they fell crashing toward the surface. Debris plummeted in every direction. Some of the podules fell and rolled about the surface like tossed marbles; some podules' exteriors split open as they smacked onto Eclipsia, sending pieces of their shells flying, curving and rolling into bits over the terrain. It was as if buildings were falling from the sky.

RamsyXan, in a brash, bold, and unprecedented move, secretly attacked CreXan's operations. By covertly destroying the vacuum craft and preventing the podules from carrying out their mining tasks, he could cause CreXan to lose profits, setting him back. RamsyXan, considering that he would be the one to one day own it all, for his own benefit thought, *what would it matter to lose a few slaves? More could always be grown.* RamsyXan already had a superior fleet of craft for this purpose, so losing these would not affect things in the long run either.

RamsyXan saw CreXan as his harshest rival and biggest obstacle, especially now that he had acquired part of Syphexan's operating system and his share of Syphexan's holdings. With CreXan voted off during the next Agglomeration, it would be an easy task to take down the other two and eventually assume total possession. With CreXan eliminated, RamsyXan felt there would be no one else to stand in his way; He would assume possession of all.

"Let's see where they landed," replied Jerish.

"Yes they may need our help."

Careful.

A sulfuric odor filled the air as ash fell. Torbot squirmed, while being partially cradled in Jerish's sweaty palms. He blinked, feeling annoyed as he tried to get the soot free from his silky eyes.

"Hey pal, you're tickling me. Stop fiddling so much."

It took some time to traverse the molten rock and make it to one of the impacted podules. A sunken orb lay melted and smoldering in the soil.

"Careful Jerish. Watch out. Those are falling hot embers."

Trails of smoky debris fell to the ground, fizzling on impact. Bits of blackened metal bounced off the terrain making clanking sounds.

Once there, Axreal cautioned, "Don't get too close. It appears to be giving off a lot of heat."

Axreal, Jerish, and Torbot then witnessed something horrific. They peered through the hatch and saw two Setiacotion bodies twisted and charred. And for a brief moment in Axreal's mind, it looked like Jerish and her own body lying crumpled and thrown together there, limbs in unnatural positions, burning.

Jerish instinctually reached out with his palms extended, "Come back!"

During their metamorphosis, their limited ability to heal their own small cuts, pains, and infections with the use of their hands had been restored to both Jerish and Axreal, but nothing could bridge the finality of death's hold.

Axreal sighed, "They didn't even know they left the factory, they didn't even know they were being taken away."

"True," remarked Jerish, sickened by the sight, "and then they were shot down like nothing."

"Are they all dead?" she asked.

"You check those over there, Torbot, and I will look into these."

After which Axreal and Jerish, with Torbot clinging to his side, swiftly ran back towards each other with their news.

Axreal spoke. "It appears they are all dead."

"It doesn't look like there's anyway any of them could have survived."

Jerish's heart swelled. He vowed, "I promise you Axreal, The System will never do anything like that to us!"

A second vacuum ship bolted into the night sky, destined for the same fate. Then a third, and then a fourth.

"We have to do something!" Axreal exclaimed.

"What can we possibly do?"

"I can breach the distance."

"It's far, and you won't even know where you'll end up inside," Jerish said.

"I can't stand by while more of our people are killed. Torbot taught us that we need each other to survive, when some of us are being misused that diminishes us all. Jerish, if they are slaughtered, part of us will be lost."

"I'll go with you!"

"NO, you have to carry out the plan we discussed. Go get Marshall and find the Haven and stop the Lam Waron."

"I'll need you to do that!"

"Look Jerish, you are going to have to do this alone, remember how far we have come, and all we are capable of. They have a right to know what we do, to experience what we have. They have a right to know their world, be it as it may. It is you who will save us; it was always meant to be you! If you succeed, our people and our world will return to dignity."

"How will you get there? How will you know where to go inside? How can you possibly do this?"

"Now who's asking all the questions? I can breach the full distance. I will have to figure, once I am inside, what to do next."

Axreal instinctively knew that having undergone the metamorphosis, she would now be able to breach more precisely. She knew it could carry her the distance she wished to go and in the direction she desired. The ability to breach had been a characteristic of Setiacotions of old, one of many abilities lost and left to waste since incorporation into The System. The ability to teleport would be unrevivable in most Setiacotions, stamped out for good, if not for Eclipsia herself. Eclipsia, in a last ditch effort, stirred inner energies and sent them to work through Jerish's and Axreal's unique circumstances to reawaken this ability in them for the purpose of their escape.

Jerish turned toward Axreal as disaster raged behind her, "How do you know you won't be reincorporated?"

"I don't, but I also don't have time to debate!" Axreal spoke fervently, having so much to care about: herself, Jerish, Torbot, Marshall, her people, and her planet. Passion had been restored in both Jerish and herself. "I will rejoin you. After I put a stop to this, I will find you! You'll need to release my hand."

Jerish released his hand hold, but not without first giving her a squeeze. Axreal stepped away from her two comrades. Torbot and Jerish looked on as Axreal appeared confident. A cascade: a hundred thousand vibrations. It began: the separation, body freed from mind, mind freed from body. A ghost. Vanishment. Axreal left them.

Jerish called after her, "Please come back in one piece." Then he turned to Torbot, "I can go in behind her!"

True, but there is a great chance she won't return, and then who will be able to carry out the plan? It is better if we find Marshall, and set out to locate the Haven.

Jerish looked over the portable scanner Marshall had given him; he had been studying it to learn its operations. Looking up from the lighted screen, his grayish blue eyes pierced into Torbot as he spoke, "I could have helped Axreal; you and I could have helped to make sure she'd return. I don't think we did the right thing."

Torbot retracted his arms to stave off the coolness of Jerish's words towards him. Logistically, he thought this was the right thing to do; their trip wouldn't be without risks.

Understand, Axreal made the best choice for herself Jerish, now we must do the same.

CreXan had been caught off guard during the torpedo attack. When The

System reported to him the destruction of the vacuum craft, he had been preoccupied with what to do about the Setiacotion's escape. And so far The System had been unable to locate them. CreXan also didn't know who was responsible for the attack. Fortunately, the Resort Haven orbited at a great distance and did not lie in the paths of the torpedoes.

The four ships of RamsyXan's automated fleet vaporized after they delivered their arsenals. They left no sign as to who sent them. They came from a Baron, that CreXan knew for sure. He would have the two escaped Setiacotions apprehended or destroyed, and he would have to discover which Baron launched the torpedoes. Once he found out who launched such a blatant attack, in extreme violation of the Barons' prior agreements, he could exact revenge.

Jerish and Torbot witnessed one other vacuum craft being launched then destroyed. Axreal would have to find a way to put a stop to the destruction and see to her own survival.

Uneasy, Jerish and Torbot made their way back to Marshall's encampment. They noticed Marshall had left no lights on onboard the ship. They did not see him about, and it was very quiet. Torbot propelled himself up to the makeshift tent ahead of Jerish. He noticed what he had expected all along: Marshall had succumbed to his illness. How should he break the news to Jerish?

Wait, Jerish.

"What is the matter pal?"

Stay, you do not need to see this. Torbot figured that maybe it would be better to just out and out tell Jerish rather than have him bluntly confront the physical remains. *Marshall is gone.*

"What do you mean? First Axreal takes off and now you tell me Marshall somehow isn't here anymore either? What I am supposed to believe next, Torbot? Huh, that he flew off in his ship?—Which is still right here!"

Understand, what is left of his body remains. But he has most assuredly gone elsewhere.

"Uh no! You're not telling me the truth, Torbot." Jerish clenched his lips around his teeth, not wishing to say anything he might regret. He fought off what reminded him of one of his tantrums. But those were clearly a thing of the past. He parted his lips enough to tell Torbot, "Let's get out of here!"

In Search of a Monster

Jerish pulled out the scanner Marshall had given him. He pointed it in every direction until the screen indicated the one in which to go.

Intelligent. You have that alien device well figured out; now what also remains is that incredible distances lie before us.

"We aren't going to be able to get there soon at this rate. I can breach part of the way but where will that leave you?"

I do desire to come along; your goals are the same as mine.

"Breaching won't be an option then, and what about food?"

Realize, the Orcadian Orangeous fruit is very potent Jerish. What you have already eaten should provide you with nourishment for a while, but it won't last anywhere near as long as our journey. That has me concerned; I don't suspect we will encounter any of the fruit outside the quarries. I do have some peels in my carryall; they will help somewhat. Other things we need to consider are hazards we might encounter, and we both will need a safe place in which to get some sleep.

"I have survived hazards before," Jerish said. "I would much rather take chances making my own decisions here than being under the control of The System. I would much rather survive out here, even if it's for only one interval. It'll be better spent than one in there. The things we were forced to do there are things no living being should ever have to face."

Certainly, I agree with you. I am sorry Jerish, that is why our mission is important. If we are successful, perhaps fewer will suffer. My people always look out for and have consideration for each other. If something doesn't feel right or is unnatural, then that is not the direction we take. We never do things that go against nature, our own or that of Eclipsia. We do not put each other in harm's way.

"I wish the early Setiacotions had been more like your people," Jerish remarked.

Perhaps they were, but they made some bad choices. Perhaps if they had been less susceptible they could have found ways to protect themselves. The ones from beyond came with superior strength though, but there still could have been a chance if they hadn't fallen for the lies and illusions.

Jerish, with Torbot springing along, moved in tandem with the scanner's indications.

"What was it like back then? Where did my people live?"

Interestingly, we have not seen anything in the way of Setiacotion villages, or dwellings. It could be they were wiped out, leveled so that nothing remained, or it could be none of us has come across them yet. Eclipsia is enormous; I don't believe we could ever cover the entire surface. We have seen no trace of the civilizations of the Kanda and Remoran either. It's almost like they were wiped off the face of Eclipsia.

"Maybe along our journey, we will find something." Jerish remained optimistic. "Here, why don't you climb up and take a rest. I'll carry you for a while."

Torbot appreciated the ride. He could, from Jerish's greater height, get a better look and keep track of what Jerish might miss off to his sides and from behind. He noticed Jerish was much stronger and his shoulders were broader. Torbot felt even safer around this new version of Jerish.

"Hey, Pal?"

Yes, Jerish.

"I am sorry I snapped at you back there with Marshall and all."

Listen, it isn't necessary to say anything. I was not offended. I miss Marshall also.

"What happens after we die—where do you suppose Marshall is?"

My people believe we go back into all that is so that we can come out as something else. We don't necessarily come back as a life form. As a scientist I have formed a hypothesis that our personalities collect on a plane, forming a collective consciousness that is the overall personality of the universe. However, I cannot run all the necessary tests, just yet, to confirm that. I believe we never entirely end. What we are gets dispersed throughout all that is; in some way, everyone that was is still here, still a part of Eclipsia now.

"So you think Marshall *is* still here also?"

Yes, somewhat. But he is also back amongst his world and his people even more so.

Jerish and Torbot continued their in-depth conversation, until deciding they needed to start looking for a safe place to sleep for the night. They had not passed anything remarkable along the way yet. They came upon a dune, of sorts, that had formed a drift against an embankment.

Perhaps, this will be suitable for a night's sleep, the skies look free of any storm activity. This will be comfortable to rest amongst. It's not a nest, but it should work.

Both laid on their backs and peered upwards. Little by little, Jerish drifted off into his first-ever natural slumber. Torbot put his mind to work, seeking solutions to their upcoming problems. His concern mostly centered on what they were supposed to do if they did encounter the Lam Warons. Torbot did not like violence; however, he did have a theory that might help them greatly.

Jerish sunk lower and lower into the sand and further into his sleep. To him, this felt a lot like being in the tubular. Images played across his mind, deeper and deeper he drifted. Torbot had not succumbed to sleep just yet. He had far too much to think about. He looked over and noticed that his Setiacotian friend was deeply asleep, but seemingly involved in something else as well.

"Is that you Axreal, did you come back?" Jerish asked the form in his dream to identify itself: "Who are you?"

For so long have I waited. All can be as it once was. Far and beyond, wondrous realities lay ahead for you. Imagine you can have everything meant for you. All is within your grasp, all can be as it was meant.

"What do you mean?"

We are together again, what was done can be undone, what was meant for you and for all can be returned.

The bright form stood back and a planetary image birthed in the center of the dream. *Eclipsia?* The planet shown as a jet black sphere with flames burning, encircling its edges. It grew until Jerish could make out the details on its surface. He saw components strewn about, the fossil bones he and Axreal had seen before, form back into the living beings they had once been. It was Eclipsia as she had been, in all her lavishness, health, and glory. It had been a paradise. The quarry life forms were but a fraction of what had been. And there were his people, living in harmony. Was this how it was once, how it was intended to be? The image vanished, and so did the bright form. The dream ended. Jerish enjoyed the rest of his natural slumber. He awoke refreshed.

Good morning, that was quite some sleep you had. It is still dark, but it is time we move forward. Share, what went on in your sleep?

"That was by far the best rest I have ever had. I thought I saw Axreal in my sleep also, but it turned out to be someone else. Ever since we first began this journey, I have often felt someone was around. I have mostly heard singing. In my sleep it was like they came to visit."

Highly interesting. It wouldn't have something to do with the oviums would it?

"No, this is clearly something from out here. What is our plan going to be now?"

Notice, Your scanner says we need to spring in that direction. It looks like the Oralean Craters.

"What is that?"

Understand, they are the border of our explored territories. They mark the edge of what we know about. They are so vast that we have never crossed them to know what is beyond. We will need to be very careful.

The land before Jerish and Torbot had symmetrical craters, some as much as half a mile long, in-between stood system fabrications that had to have served some mining purpose before. Now they looked like abandoned wreckages. What larger purpose they served was not known. Very little of what the Lam Warons did made sense. Jerish noticed strange substances impacted in the craters. A blue electrical charge streaked between two of the wreckages. Something here was still semi-operational.

While taking steps into the first crater, they noticed certain impacted materials gave way and fell, making the area treacherous to traverse.

Perhaps, it would be better to hike along the ridges, just so long as we avoid those buildings. Let's also try not to slip.

"I think you are right!" Jerish half-expected to reach for Axreal's hand. How was she and what was she doing?

That took a lot of courage, Jerish thought, to do what she did. He would need to be that courageous also.

The fabrications had all kinds of mechanizations within them. They seemed to have served numerous functions. Maybe they served to collect energy from the craters below. Their numerous metals gave off a very negative and twisted smell.

Torbot reached into his carryall. He pulled out a dried fruit peel for Jerish to snack on. He took notice of Jerish's bushy brown eyebrows as Jerish turned his neck to peer at his passenger.

A blast erupted as electricity shot out in beams from all of the wreckage buildings, knocking Jerish and Torbot out.

When they both came to, their heads ached and they saw the strangest sight towering above them.

Worried. Are you alright?

"Yep, I seem okay, Torbot. What are those? Are they alive?"

Certainly not. They must be devices from the oviums.

Above them, trudging like gigantic, thin walking sticks, The System's cargo striders carried materials to the processing facilities. Cargo holds hung from what served as their bellies. They had such a huge reach that their thin, coppery legs could stretch over the craters. With their cargo aboard, they made their way to the processing facilities. This was just one more bizarre manifestation of the Lam Warons' system. They did everything in unnatural ways.

After the six-legged striders passed, Jerish and Torbot proceeded on their way.

"I hope we don't have to go through that again!"

The area grew hot, and Jerish pulled off his shirt. Perspiration dripped down his sides.

Listen, what if you breach to see what lays ahead for us?

"That is a great idea. There seems to be no end in sight to this place. Maybe I can see a place where this will end sooner, and we can be out of here faster!"

Jerish started to create a breach , which were much easier to undergo now and did not require a tantrum to initiate. Tantrums seemed to be a thing of the past and happened mostly in the processing facilities.

The process began: A hundred thousand revolutions. He blurred into the background; left behind was an afterimage. A ghost. Vanishment. Then he returned to bring news to Torbot.

Tell. What did you see?

"It took a few breaches to get there, but the last craters are a good hundred miles out. They converge upon what I think are mountain ranges. It doesn't look like it's going to get any easier."

It is too bad we could not hitch a ride on one of those striders if we could find one going that direction even.

"Whul. Why can't we?" Jerish said. "I think that may just be the answer."

CreXan determined, "I, the greatest and finest Lam Waron, must stop the Setiacotion escapees. They pose a severe threat being loose. Another attack by torpedoes is unlikely and The System will not be caught off guard as before. Defenses are fully in place for that. Something must be done."

CreXan activated his new miniature portable interface. He had it made to accompany him everywhere. Even in the presence of others, only he could see and hear it. That way he could be kept constantly apprised by The System and could more quickly enter his instructions. A pink holographic window remained on the side of his face to accept commands.

CreXan rode his resort skid in haste, speeding down numerous descending corridors until the skid came to a vault. The vault held the accumulated knowledge and history, an encyclopedia, of all Lam Waron experience. CreXan sought to find out what, if anything, it would reveal about what to do in the event of a Setiacotion leak from the Eclipsian processing facilities.

CreXan weighed his options. "I could use the anesthetizing gasses the early Harvesters used to knock out the three species when we first captured them from the surface. However, those poisons were procured on Lam Waron Prime ages ago, and it might require too much time for The System to make the quantities needed. The poisons used for the new manufacturing world would not work the same here. CreXan then happened upon something that stood out from the electronic pages. "AMAZING!" CreXan squealed at the data depicted in front of him.

The encyclopedia revealed a hibernating subclass of engineered Lam Waron. They had once served as an offensive army at a time when numerous Lam Warons fought for control of Eclipsia.

"If they still exist, I can revive them and have them comb the surface for the Axreal and Jerish malformations within seconds. My, I do look grand!" CreXan stated as he caught sight of his appearance while considering his magnificent discovery.

CreXan called upon The System. He entered the ancient voice commands the encyclopedia directed him to use to see if The System could connect with the hibernating Lam Goria. Once it found them, it began to initialize them. Each Lam Goria shook in its underground capsule. The capsules lay strategically buried in graves all over Eclipsia.

The Lam Goria's joints creaked from thousands of years of disuse. They had served numerous Barons during upheavals. Up until now, they remained encrypted, as there had not been any rival Lam Warons on Eclipsia in hundreds of years that used armies against each other. CreXan had no need of an army himself until now.

The System also presented CreXan with a portrait of his new chief Kanda drudge. He panted.

"My, she beats Lorese all talons in the air! It is about time I revisit Lorese and see how she is getting along. Eeeeeeeee!" His high-pitched squeal nearly caused the vault's gold paint to flake off. He let out a discharge.

CreXan returned to his major concern. He ordered The System, "I COMMAND YOU: program all Lam Goria to emerge, begin hunting for Setiacotion escapees, and destroy them without delay. Keep me, Supreme Majesty CreXan, informed directly and immediately."

The System had no trouble sending out the microwave signals to activate the Lam Goria all across Eclipsia's globe. Overall, about three hundred Lam Goria rose to reactivation. Thousands could no longer respond, as time had worn them inoperable. Some Lam Goria emerged from dump heaps and wasting pools, and a couple had even broken through to take off from the midst of Torbot's colony. A dozen had emerged at the Oralean Craters.

"Torbot!" Jerish stated, alarmed.

Listening. What is it Jerish? Torbot was still recovering from his headache.

"Look. What in all torment is that?"

Jerish drew Torbot's attention to the depths below. An eruption broke through the odd substances of the crater nearest to them.

Suggestion. We need to locate one of those striders now, and get out of here!

"I'm with you on that one, pal! Get back on!"

Rising from the infernal heat of the Oralean Craters, two Lam Goria hibernators undertook their orders. They had three modified and elongated rear appendages. They served as three strong legs so that they could run upright, rather than low to the ground. A machine armor encased their transparent, slender would-be torsos. Slitted eyes peered out from steal masks. Lam Goria had been so greatly modified that they could not be considered Lam Warons. Lam Goria had been clearly engineered for fighting.

Torbot instilled, *We'll need to go in this direction.* A number of his sticky gel arms pointed in the direction he had last seen the copper striders go in.

"There's one now!" Jerish exclaimed while running. The pastel shirt Torbot's people had given him was tied about his waist. He did not miss his confining system fatigues at all. He only wished that he could have shredded them to bits or burned them in a fire.

Catching up to a cargo conveyer would be difficult, getting aboard one of its legs would be a major challenge. However, they seemed to have no other options.

Suggestion. Jerish we won't be able to catch up to it, but there is another conveyor coming up from behind. We should figure out where it is most likely to step. If we wait there, then we can latch onto its leg. Then we can climb aboard.

"They are walking pretty uniformly. I bet they step where the previous one does!"

Good thinking, let's get there fast.

Both Jerish and Torbot awaited the cargo strider's massive footstep. Jerish climbed up its foot. Torbot leapt up and secured Jerish and himself to the strider's shining leg. He stretched some of his gel arms around Jerish and it, then formed a knot to secure them.

Notice, Torbot imparted, *we can stay fixed like this till we can jump off. Whatever those were back there, they'll have a hard time catching up!*

Great surprise overtook Jerish and Torbot as the massive "walking stick" approached the mountain range.

"Torbot!" Jerish said. "Look, it's going to carry us over the mountains!"

Wonderful, it is about time we had some good luck! Jerish are you still reading Lam Waron signatures?

Jerish pulled Marshall's portable scanner from his pocket.

"Yes, Torbot, but it is growing fainter as we get closer. I don't understand. Shouldn't it be getting stronger the closer we get to it?"

I would agree with that determination. Perhaps something is wrong with the scanner?

As the copper strider made its trek across the mountains, boulders and hillsides fell way under its step. Torbot and Jerish grew sore from having to hold on so tightly.

"Even if it is malfunctioning, we will need to get off here. The walker is heading away from the signature now! I am going to jump off. Hold tight, Torbot."

Jerish leapt off the great courier's foot. Torbot rolled around to Jerish's back as Jerish landed on his stomach. His hands stretched out before him, flat against the ground. Looking up and ahead of them, he saw a vast yellow-orange ocean. The smell made Jerish grow sick.

Torbot had rolled off Jerish's unclad back, diving into the acid waters.

"Torbot!" Jerish yelled after him. Jerish received a response before Torbot got out too far.

Wait, I am going out to see if I can find the Resort Haven. Understand, you cannot enter the waters—they are dangerous to you. They will most likely eat right through you. Stay back behind the boulders. If a breeze starts, head back up into the mountains and I will find you. As long as it is calm, you will be safe.

Jerish felt frightened and put his shirt back on. *What if a breeze kicks up and sends the acid towards me? How is it that Torbot can withstand it? If Torbot finds the Resort Haven, how on Eclipsia will I be able to get there? We'll have to find another way to get through the sea, maybe with a raft, and how will we be able to get aboard the Haven?*

Jerish's mind raced until Torbot returned.

Understand, Jerish, there is no sign of what Marshall described. The reason the scanner was faint is that perhaps the Lam Waron were here and have since left. Or maybe something is wrong with the device and they were never here at all. I tend to think they were here—as the scanner grew faint, they departed.

"Where did they go?"

Recall. Marshall told us that the Lam Warons lived in huge floating mansions. They can move them, even take off in them to locate to other worlds. Perhaps this one took off.

"Whul, that is just great. What are we supposed to do now?"

After Jerish spoke, the breeze picked up.

Caution, Jerish. Right now we need to get you back from the acid water.

From above, a small vessel descended.

"Whul, The System has us!"

Observe, we do not know that yet.

"You're right. We must see everything through to the end, and never be willing to give up."

The ACS set down on the shore. Its legs sunk into the sand. The lapping sea waves it stirred soon settled down. A woven hatch unfurled from the Lam Waron vessel.

"Torbot, it's Axreal!"

Axreal spoke. "Jerish! Torbot! What are you waiting for? Get aboard!"

Concern, Jerish let us confirm that it is her. Torbot noticed something different about her and then he imparted solely to Axreal: *So where is the medallion Marshall gave you?*

Axreal peered across the shore and met Jerish's smoky blue eyes. The metamorphosis had not removed, from within them, all of life's sadness. She could clearly see he had missed her as well.

"It is me! See, here. I took the medallion off for safekeeping. It's been in my pocket."

Torbot, having gotten her reply to his implanted thought message, knew she could not be an entire illusion.

Next Torbot sent a thought message to Jerish, *It appears to be her, but we do not know if the ones from beyond are using her image to lure us.* Then he imparted to all, *Listen. If you are Axreal, we need to know for certain and that you are acting independently of having been in the oviums. Step out of the vessel and allow me to board.* Then to Jerish alone he imparted, *Understand, if she is willing to surrender the vehicle to us, then she can be trusted. We need to know that nothing else is aboard with her, though. Axreal, is there anyone else on board the vessel?*

"No, Torbot, there's no one else. It flies itself. No one was aboard when I discovered it. I am able to direct it, though. I will step out and you and Jerish can look into it."

Jerish, you remain behind. I will see if what she says is true. If the ship was sent here to capture us, I do not see how they'd let me have control over it.

Torbot leapt into the ACS. He found the controls easy to operate just as Axreal had indicated.

Outside Jerish hesitated to approach Axreal until Torbot confirmed everything.

"Whul, what's your conclusion, Torbot?" he said.

Torbot looked down from the hatch.

Be aware, there is no one else in here. Everything seems okay, however we need a lot more explanation from Axreal. Torbot vacated the ACS and joined Jerish.

"What happened?" Jerish eagerly turned towards Axreal, wanting to know the details.

"Did you get back to Marshall?" Axreal was also anxious to find out what they had been up to.

"First tell us, Axreal, what went on with you, and then we'll tell you what happened to us!"

"Okay," she acquiesced. "I breached through the barriers of the processing facilities. I found myself suspended above thousands of podules, midair. I was so stunned, scared, and jolted. They rolled around each other as they worked frantically below me constructing something. A vast object emerged out from between them. They scurried around it while making adjustments to it. It looked, from what I gathered, like a giant engine. I was able to see podules descending, off to the side. They poured out from above, where the connectways ended, and fell below. I got a glimpse of a few of our people as they fell alongside me. They looked numbed and pale. Terror registered on their faces, but not in their actions. I saw one Setiacotion female, wired and locked into her workstation. It was awful Jerish. Her hands had been moving so fast to do her work that they were red and bleeding, and she didn't even know it!"

Torbot let out a squeak. He had not had a mental picture of the inside of oviums before. Jerish listened with rapt attention.

"I breached again in a hurry, or I'd have plummeted to my death. I tried my best to figure out where I was and to get to somewhere safer. I recognized several sites. I had to dodge jets of bioaltering gasses. They tried to weaken me, and I had to prevent myself from being reincorporated. I knew if I just kept moving, The System couldn't apprehend me. Luckily, I recognized what resembled the ships that we saw launching from the processing facilities. Many more were being prepared. I thought that maybe I could do something to prevent their launch. I breached inside one and began to hit every switch I could to disrupt it. I was successful. It stayed in place and I got out of it. Then I noticed the rest of the ships collected about a pad. The pad flipped over with all of the ships attached, and they disappeared. No more were sent into the launch tower after that."

Jerish said, "After you left, we saw only one other ship destroyed, then we turned to find Marshall. Looking back, I didn't hear or see anything else. Marshall was no longer alive when we found him."

"I am sorry to hear that," responded Axreal.

Jerish continued, "It was difficult to leave you. I hoped you'd be successful at stopping the launches. Whul, to be truthful I don't think we ever expected to see you again." His hands cupped Axreal's shoulders and he pulled her towards him in an embrace. "I am glad you made it. Just please don't go off in such a hurry without us again!" They each felt a warmth centered about their hearts at being reunited.

"I'm not sure I can promise that, but I'll try." Then referring to their embrace, Axreal commented, "You've never done this before."

"It seemed like the best time to do so. Whul, anyways, what did you do next?" Jerish released her.

"I wasn't sure what to do next. I just wanted to get out of there. That's when I discovered this vessel. I had breached upon it, and from its displays, I noticed it leaving the processing facilities. I learned I could direct it. I decided to ride out with it and to go in search of you. When left alone, it will resume its directed course. Have you found the Lam Waron Haven?"

"Marshall's scanner directed us here. Torbot swam out to where it should have been. It appears to have taken off. We were being followed," he said as he saw Axreal's concern, "by some sort of three-legged attackers. They had maskings, steal armor, and thin-slitted eyes."

"Where are they now?" asked Axreal.

Understand, they came out of the ground at the craters some distance back. They could not catch up with us, but that does not mean they are not on their way here now.

"Maybe we better get aboard then. The vessel was on its way here; left alone it appears to want to go back. The System is going to want it back! Maybe we can figure some way to use it for our advantage."

"The scanner is not detecting any other Lam Waron signatures right now. I don't know how we are going to locate them," Jerish replied.

"Maybe, we don't have to," Axreal said.

"What do you mean?" Jerish replied.

"Maybe we can enter The System and get some of them out using this vessel. Maybe there is a way together we can set the Setiacotions and Remoran free."

Jerish responded, "Torbot, hadn't you mentioned that there were three species altogether that got incorporated?"

Yes, that is correct.

"I don't know anything about a third one. Perhaps we will encounter them," spoke Axreal.

Perhaps, imparted Torbot.

"Whul, that is just one of the processing facilities," replied Jerish, "There are many, many more."

"True, but with others freed we might be able to work together to shut down the entire system," Axreal answered.

"They will need to undergo the metamorphosis for us to know if any of them can breach. That will take time. They'll be like us when we first came out. Remember how limited our capabilities were?" spoke Jerish.

Yes, instilled Torbot, *but they are no longer. You both have accomplished and learned very much.*

"We could start them undergoing it," said Axreal.

Realize, they may have other abilities once they come out from the tubulars' encasements. Things we might not even know about.

"Those may also be of use," said Jerish. "Whul, the sooner we get some others out, the sooner they can undergo the transformation."

At that moment, four Lam Goria hibernators came charging along the shore! They aimed weapons!

"Get aboard," ordered Axreal. "We are out of here!"

The Lam Goria fired what appeared to be a gas mixture confined to a twelve-inch-circumference beam. The beam widened as it extended outward.

Torbot boarded last. His glowing gel body flew through the hatch as the door wove shut.

A beam from the Lam Goria encompassed a good portion of the ACS. A second later and it would have pulverized Torbot. The vessel sped away towards the nearest processing facility.

The miniature portable interface diligently kept CreXan apprised of the Lam Goria's actions. With it, The System indicated that the Lam Goria had chased one of the Setiacotion escapees, the male, to the acid sea, with some sort of multiarmed gel creature. There they met up with the female, who had been located previously at sporadic points within the processing facilities. She was never at these points long enough for capture, and where she was between points was not known either. She'd ridden out in an ACS.

"That malformation was looking to get aboard my beautiful resort! Where are they now?"

The System responded, "Setiacotions and gel creature are currently located aboard vehicle. Apprehension plans now under way."

"Follow them, find out where they are going, set traps for them, and stop at nothing to destroy them!" CreXan ordered.

CreXan then sat back in his newly upholstered sofa. The escape had him worried and the situation started to tire him. One of his eyes registered the miniature interface. The other kept an eye on the burly Kanda replacing the glass mirror Lorese had so rudely scratched.

CreXan remained safe from the Kanda, which attended so closely to him. However, it did not hurt to keep one eye on them. Each Kanda, while developing in the Remoran nurseries, was implanted with a Chem-Pac. If a Kanda ever did anything to warrant CreXan's wrath, by use of his commands he could cause the Chem-Pac to burst. It would release poisons into the Kanda's body, thus killing him or her. For that reason CreXan never feared those closest to him, the drudges. He could have burst Lorese's Chem-Pac and been done with her. But where would the fun be in doing that?

CreXan considered to himself, *By the way, it is time to take a little look in on my little conspirator. I am safe from the Kanda. As for those damn malformations and that creature, I don't know.* He got inspired, *Maybe it is time to put an end to the occupation of Eclipsia. I never did like this rock very much. I have been here far too long. I have just about used her up. But alas, I will have to wait till everything is ready on the new manufacturing world. The System is harvesting the slaves as I speak. Factory installations have been dropped into place. There is only one higher-brain carrier set for incorporation. That should make the whole system run more smoothly!*

CreXan rode his skid to Lorese's quarters.

"O Wonderful, Rightful Leader of the Serendipity," Lorese managed enough strength to address CreXan in the proper tone.

"You need not continue with the pleasantries. I am here to inform you that I, Great and Wonderful Leader of all, have replaced you. She is quite stunning. Why, you are looking downright famished."

"Why not just be done with it? There's that Chem-Pac thing you've used."

"Oh, but that would be all too easy. Aren't you the least bit curious why I am doing this to you?"

"Not really," Lorese realized she was being kept close to death and had little left to lose, so she remarked, "You heinous monster!"

"So you ugly Kanda drudge, you are finally speaking your mind. Good for you. However, it really will not do you any good now. Just like this won't," he hurled Lorese's feathered sprucer back at her. "Seems you tried to help two Setiacotions get past The System and myself, briefly. They are meddling below on the surface. I have resurrected an ancient Lam Waron army, which is presently seeking to destroy them. I am very close to relocating and will not need the Eclipsian processing facilities any longer. I may just go ahead and move the Resort to the new planet. You'll get to see it after all!" He stuck a brown nodule onto one of his fangs, much like an olive on a toothpick. "All this visiting with you has made me tired."

With that, CreXan squealed out an order, "Risase, my new chief Kanda drudge, attend to me now! PREPARE A MUD TREATMENT! I want my snack foods from the celebrations brought to me!"

The lights went out and Lorese sat in complete darkness.

Meanwhile, Axreal and Jerish stood, peering out from the ACS's poorly lit control cabin. Torbot adhered to the ceiling, dangling by one of his sticky gel arms. An ominous clanking echoed from behind them. Torbot swung back and forth as Axreal and Jerish slammed into the sides of the ACS. Torbot lost his sticky grip from the ceiling and plummeted, landing atop them.

Attention, attention, Torbot imparted. *The vessel is changing course.*

The contents of the ACS rocked back and forth noisily until the ACS leveled off.

The commotion settled and Torbot rolled off of Jerish so that Jerish could stand. Once upright, Jerish grasped Axreal's arm and helped her stand up. The commotion left each of them banged up. Torbot had to once again thank his protective padding for softening the blows.

"Whew, hope that doesn't happen again!" Jerish said.

"Let's find out where we are," Axreal spoke.

Notice, we are not the only ones aboard either.

Torbot redirected their attention to the Lam Goria that stood behind them. Parts of its modified face pressed through its overlaying maskings and boiled, seemingly in rage. Its would-be chest, presumably its lungs, rose and fell in exasperated gasps.

Jerish noticed it had a sickening negative odor.

The Lam Goria hibernator's left and right legs moved forward together. Its middle leg helped support it from behind. From its slitted mouth, it spit a net, which fell and hardened around Axreal and Jerish.

Torbot made his way back up to the ceiling and squeezed into a recess. He worked to pull himself further inwards, and his sticky gel arms held him in place. The stars of the Serendipity reflected off the control panel revealing that the ACS flew above the murky atmosphere.

The Lam Goria stowaway had attached itself to the vessel; by entering its pass code it slipped through the loading hatch. Next, it had purposefully confused the ship's course, sending it spiraling upward, just beyond the atmosphere. Now it acted ready to carry out its programming to completion.

Axreal, anxious and frightened, struggled with nausea at the sight of their intruder. She listened as Jerish spoke, "We can get out of this easily enough."

Emancipating the Slaves

The Lam Goria stowaway trusted that Jerish and Axreal would not be able to get out from its net. That annoying gel creature had to be somewhere around, but that did not matter. The Lam Goria approached the controls to set the ship to destruct.

Axreal spoke, "What is your plan, Jerish?"

"Whul, it's easy for us to breach from the net. Then we may be able to jump it. With our combined weight we could slam into it and push it out the hatchway. With the hatch closed it'd be stuck outside, and we could breach back aboard."

Torbot imparted, *Careful, you may not be aware, but we seem to be up above the atmosphere. Opening the hatch could be very dangerous; we do not know what it consists of out there.*

The Lam Goria remained too occupied with making its settings to be able to hear their plans.

Jerish called up to Torbot, "You remain inside. Open the hatch as we hit it. Once we are outside, seal the hatch shut. She and I can breach back aboard and then we can get out of here."

Axreal spoke, "Lets try it. I will count . . . When I say 'Three,' we'll breach, and Torbot, you be ready at the hatch to open and close it. One, two, three."

With the net now vacated, Axreal and Jerish ran full body weight into the Lam Goria. Torbot opened the hatch. Axreal, Jerish, and the Lam Goria hurdled into space. Then Torbot sealed the hatch.

In the chill of space, the Lam Goria thrust his appendages about. He failed in a furious attempt to gain hold of Axreal and Jerish.

"Jerish, there's no breathable air! Breach back now!" Axreal yelled.

The Lam Goria, with the cold constricting its veins, tumbled in the weightlessness of space.

Jerish and Axreal breached back aboard, falling to the deck. Their skin had chapped and they gasped for air. Torbot hit the control throttle as far forward as it could go. He had observed Axreal using this to direct the ACS and he knew doing so would speed them away. The five distant stars of Ashton's Belt sped in a line across the viewport.

Brilliant—another well executed plan! Torbot imparted.

"What should we do now? We have this ship. We can go back and get our people like we had planned, or we can search for the Haven." Axreal said. "Jerish do you have any readings on it?"

Jerish grasped Marshall's portable device. "There is a reading, but it is very, very faint. Axreal–it's, it's got to be faaarrr."

Attention. My thoughts are important in this matter, Torbot imparted.

Jerish and Axreal turned towards him.

Jerish said, "Sorry pal, what is it?"

Be aware, the vessel may not have enough energy to go that far.

Axreal spoke, "Torbot's right. The fuel levels are lowering."

"We should get to the surface then," replied Jerish. "It will just take us longer to find the Lam Waron Haven! That's all." He safely placed Marshall's scanner into his pants pocket.

"I'll go ahead and get us headed back to the surface. Everyone get secured," spoke Axreal.

The ACS dove down through the atmosphere's turbulence and landed on a plateau above the rock beds. Fossil bones, undisturbed for thousands of years, crumbled, flew off, and turned to dust as the vessel's legs made contact with the surface.

Torbot pulled from his carryall the last two pieces of Orcadian Orangeous peels, *Axreal, Jerish . . . Here, have this to eat.*

In between bites Jerish remarked, "How are we going to get our people out?"

Axreal swallowed then responded, "We will need the vessel to transport them out. However, I am not entirely sure how we will get them out of their podules, short of breaking into them. But wait . . . I do know where we can find some people already out of their podules! But they will be injured, and some might still be acting out their programming."

"Whul, where do you mean, and whul, why would they be injured?"

"Do you remember the retractable arm I used to have?"

"Yes," replied Jerish.

"When I was injured, I was shuttled to a Remoran lab. Working there is a technician, Etrabell. I never actually saw him. But he did speak to me. He engineered the retractable arm for me. Doing so, he explained to me, saved me from disposal. He tries to fix as many injured as he can. By making enhancements, he convinces The System that the slave is worthy of saving. If he can't do so, then the slave is disposed of. Most are. I know we will find others there and I know how to find the lab. He may be of some help."

"How can we rescue them if they are injured?"

"Some will have nearly recovered from their enhancement operations and still be out of their podules. Those are the ones we can get out," Axreal replied.

We will have to fly them to the quarry colonies where my people can tend to them. Given some time to rest and heal, they will then be ready to undergo the metamorphosis, Torbot instilled.

"They'll come out restored whole, like we did!" said Axreal.

"You're right! They should," replied Jerish.

"Etrabell, might be able to fix up any that are injured long enough for us to deliver them to the quarries," Axreal spoke. "How many should we try to free at first?"

The swelling sensation in Jerish's chest rose up as he replied, "My heart tells me as many as we can!"

Axreal said, "I agree." Then turning to Torbot, she asked, "How many can the tubulars accommodate?"

Realize, each of the tubulars can hold up to four Setiacotions at a time. There are, in my rough estimation, forty mature tubular plants. So one-hundred-sixty Setiacotions can undergo the transformation at the same time. If we free more, they can simply wait to undergo the process.

"Whul, that still doesn't explain how we move them to the vessel," Jerish wondered.

"Etrabell might be able to assist with that as well," Axreal replied.

"Also, Axreal, how will I be able to find the lab?"

"I'll describe what to look for and where to go."

"I wish there was a way we could breach together."

"If we head in the same direction and stay in the breach for the same duration we should end up in the same spot."

"Yeah but if we are slightly off we could be separated. I could end up inside a reactor or within a wall."

"I don't think so. When I was in the processing facility, if I found that was about to happen, I merely stayed breaching until I formed somewhere safe. If you get lost, just keep looking for the things I will describe to you. We will eventually meet up," said Axreal.

After making their plans, Axreal drove the ACS close to where it could resume its preprogrammed course back within the processing facility. They stood in quiet contemplation of the difficult tasks before them. As the vessel got closer, so did the flashes of eerie blue luminance. Noise and vibration rattled the vessel as it approached the processing facility's outermost wall. An entryway shaped like a giant mouth opened before them. It had previously been nonexistent. Its mechanized lips engulfed the vessel and consumed it within.

Jerish lowered himself to be level with Torbot, "Come here, pal. I know you want to come all the way with us. But it is not necessary, and we do not think it is even possible. You need to remain aboard the ACS. We'll bring the rescued back and get them on board. Be ready to help fly us out."

Meanwhile back aboard the Resort Haven, The System called for CreXan's immediate attention: "WARNING. Lam Goria Hibernators Deactivated, Setiacotions and Unknown Entering Plantech Processing Facility 3." Its monotonous, loud voice and blaring, florescent-pink warning startled the pompous Lam Waron from his grooming session.

Risase lost CreXan's ornate talon scissors, as CreXan yanked his appendages away from where she had been clipping his nails. The scissors flew, nearly hitting her in the face. Their clanking echoed as they hit the floor. They came to rest a few feet away.

"ENOUGH," CreXan ordered his entertainment monitor to turn off and he squealed further. "Clear all of this away!" he blasted at the Kanda waiters to take away his current feasts and the accompanying gaudy decorations. "I can't be distracted by all this now!"

The drudges mindlessly obeyed and reset the dining area to its prior state. The Kanda, massaging his feet, halted. They collected the exotic massage oil and richly textured towels, bowing as they departed.

CreXan hated disruptions while imbibing the Gelaguise. Gelaquise consisted of aromatic therapies, mood altering substances, and muscle relaxants. CreXan always enjoyed it while watching his entertainment monitor.

CreXan shook violently, so much so that his interface flickered.

"Why aren't my Lam Goria warriors responding?" CreXan demanded.

The portable interface displayed the demise of the remainder of the Lam Goria. Their *living* bodies had sustained them until decay fully overtook them and they could go no further.

"Eeehhh," CreXan continued in outrage. "System, use any means to kill the escaped Setiacotions and that unknown. If all attempts fail, ignite Plantech Processing Facility 3. I will not allow any malformations to disrupt my operations. Anyways, the processing facilities on Obscuria are ready to take over for Plantech 3. The consumer world's orders must in no way be delayed!"

"Beautiful, Handsome, Supreme Ruler of All, Your Graceful Benevolence, do not trouble yourself. All will be done to see your wishes fulfilled, Your Majesty. It is the purpose of your humble Kanda and your System to do thy will to perfection," Risase spoke, curtsying with each sentiment of praise.

"That is more like it!" CreXan remarked. Then he thought, Lorese never did that well, even on her best interval. There's not even a hint of jealousy in her voice, like in the way Lorese spoke. CreXan told Risase, "Come closer."

As Risase approached him, she did not let on that his odor bothered her. Perhaps the Remorans designed her with immunity and she certainly had improved programming. Also, Risase's duties as chief Kanda drudge did not need to be as extensive as Lorese's.

CreXan retracted the folds of flesh about his mouth and released his fangs. He pressed them into Risase's mottled cheek, just enough to cause a little pain and not enough to puncture the skin—a Lam Waron kiss.

"We must always kiss this way," CreXan spoke.

Risase replied, "I will be so honored." Then she thought, *How nice, you are so caring.*

Risase went about resuming her programmed duties while CreXan addressed his miniature interface. "Notify ration procurement to reduce production by fifty percent, and reduce all rations to the Setiacotions, Remorans, and Kanda, by half as well, except for Risase. Operations will be winding down soon, so there is no sense wasting resources by feeding the slaves the same. Notify the other Barons that RamsyXan has attacked—in extreme violation of our accords—the Lam Waron operations on Eclipsia. His ships torpedoed five *vacuum craft* out of Eclipsia's sky on their way to gather resources on Urxis Minor. I demand that RamsyXan be held accountable."

CreXan had determined that only RamsyXan could be capable of such a transgression. *He has launched torpedo attacks at previous Barons in the past. He has established patterns of using them. It could only have been him. I must notify the others! First, I will alert them to the possibility that they may come under such an attack, and second, this will go a long way to lower RamsyXan's standing at the next Wamp Agglomeration.*

CreXan squealed as he noticed the mud's residue between some of his nodules. "Risase, continue doing my massage for me. They did not remove all of the mud treatment! CITMOP! It is time for more CITMOP!"

Back within Plantech 3, the ACS had lowered its legs and set down onto a loading bay.

"We have to be quick about this. Follow my directions closely, Jerish," Axreal said. She did not wish for them to depart, so she held firmly to her last image of Jerish.

The lights of the control panel increasingly shook faster and faster in front of Axreal's eyes. They became a blur, then Axreal closed her eyes. She began to vibrate and convulse with a hundred thousand vibrations. It began. Axreal blurred into the background. Left behind was an afterimage. A ghost. Vanishment. A successful breach.

Shortly thereafter, Jerish also breached. However, in his case, the lights of the control panel increasingly sped faster and faster in front of his eyes. They became a blur, then Jerish closed his eyes and he extended his arms out for balance. He spun in place with a hundred thousand revolutions. It began. Jerish blurred into the background, left behind was an afterimage. A ghost. Vanishment. A successful breach.

Like always, Torbot watched in amazement as they left. Next, he noticed the ACS starting to behave strangely. He grew scared and sprung into the recess above for safety.

Why are the walls moving like that? Torbot wondered. *Attention, Attention, Jerish, Axreal, there is something very wrong going on in here!*

However, it was too late. Jerish and Axreal had already traveled out of range. A loud screeching rattled the vessel.

Torbot thought, *Hopefully, I will survive this and be able to get back to the nest and Ator someday soon.*

The scene of the ACS's control cabin began to distort as if everything had somehow turned into waves of liquid. Solid, stationary matter was no more. His own body was contorting with the fluctuating waves.

Then a wall consisting of varying blue lights moved across the interior. Its flaring edges traced the ship's contours, melting them with intense heat.

Torbot rotated himself around and faced his protective padding outward to seal himself deep inside the metallic and wired recess. The wall of light passed over him and singed across the exposed parts of his body.

Ooooohhh, he squeaked in anguish. *They knew we were coming and they planned to cook us aboard the vehicle!*

His protection lasted through the blistering wall of light as it made three more passes and then it turned off. The walls along with everything else, including Torbot's gel body, returned to a more normal solid state.

With hesitation, Torbot painfully moved out from the recess to peer into the rest of the vessel. Smoke rose from the controls. The entire control panel lay in a melted, goopy mess. The viewport had shrunk. A gigantic arm picked up the ACS and threw it down a connectway.

Axreal appeared at the generator she had described to Jerish as the point where they would first meet. She stood atop a flat, cold, dark metallic circle. Below and off to its sides an immense machine turbine spun. If she had come completely out of the breach and far off the mark, the turbine's blades would have sliced her to death! The same would hold true for Jerish.

Axreal waited a few seconds for Jerish. She had just enough time to notice how different The System was since the last time she was here: There were far more sounds and activity; it smelled far worse; and it felt more threatening. The vast compartment she stood within filled with bioaltering gasses. They caught up in the turbine and soon they filled the entire scene.

"Jerish, get here now!" Axreal screamed and coughed out her plea.

From out of the cloud of gas mixtures instead came plodropeds, tiny flying robots about an inch in length. The System normally used them to make repairs in cramped places or to make deliveries to hard-to-reach areas. They served as messengers and deliverers. Now they saturated the factories. The System programmed them to assault any unaccounted-for, free-roaming Setiacotions. They had sludge-colored blinking "eyes" and they stapled themselves all over Axreal.

Axreal waved her hands over her naturally pale yellow skin and her recycled cloth garment. Her healing powers were enough to dislodge the intruders. One of them she had a hard time getting at, though. It made its way beneath the ringlets of her hair and embedded itself tightly in her scalp.

Axreal frantically tried to dislodge the plodroped before it entered her body. The gasses had somehow made her skin permeable to them. They carried packs of Tee-adrine ready to liquefy her and Jerish.

Jerish finally appeared through the haze a few feet off to her side.

"Don't remain! Breach to the next points! And get to the lab," she yelled out.

The smoke muffled her words, but Jerish could still understand them.

A swarm of the tiny flying plodropeds also collected in a circle about Jerish. They flew off him as he quickly spun to the next location.

Axreal managed to dislodge the plodroped and breached.

Jerish followed the directions Axreal had given him. He was to head downward at a forty-five-degree angle from there for a specified length of time. There he should encounter the conveyers, from the conveyers it was but a short distance to the next point and to the Remoran lab.

When Jerish breached to his next meeting point, his heart raced at the sight of Axreal. She'd gotten ahead of him. There she stood in place as if trapped. Jerish glided his hands over her and felt terror. She was not blinking; it was as if she had been turned into a statue.

"Axreal, what has happened?" said Jerish.

There came no response from the hardened form standing before him. He rested his hand over his heart. He looked quickly around for any sign as to what may have occurred. Above, vast highways of podules sped the slaves to their labors. Below, the conveyers carried packaged goods of all shapes and sizes to be loaded for delivery, the Lam Waron Universal Conglomerates insignia proudly displayed on them.

Something is happening to her from within, he thought.

A war did rage deep in Axreal's consciousness.

Within her mind, the voice of The System fought to take her over. Through reincorporation, it sought to carry out CreXan's mandate. It repeated continuously, "I am nothing; I belong only to The System. There is nothing but The System. I can only exist as part of The System. I do what I am instructed or I will accept punishment." As that played continuously in the background of her awareness, The System sought to erase her memories and to rewrite her personality. It also attempted to wipe out all of her records of ever having been out on the surface or ever having known Jerish and Torbot. The System also burned into her: "There is no escape, I will obey all protocols, I accept punishment." She heard her own voice willingly making the statements along with it.

Axreal fought for herself, speaking, "I am Axreal, I have purpose, I am my own person, I can make choices for myself, I am Axreal, I have purpose . . ."

Jerish sensed that Axreal was tied up with some sort of inner turmoil. Then he realized, "Axreal, it's The System. Fight it, don't let it take you!"

Axreal heard faintly Jerish's voice. It helped her in the fight, as did his grasping of her hand.

"Jerish, is that you? Are you there? Where's Torbot?"

"I'm here. Torbot's waiting for us. We have to get out of here. We must get to Etrabell. Axreal come back. You can do it. Do not let it have you! Do not believe anything it says."

The System intensified its attacks. Pressure built inside Axreal's skull as The System attacked her cerebral cortex. Images of factory life surrounded by illusions played out across her awareness. She felt nearly convinced to surrender to The System.

Axreal fended for herself and began speaking, "I am Axreal, I–I belong–I have purpose, I do what I am instructed, NO, NO, that's not true. That is a lie! I will *not* accept punishment, you cannot have me, you will never own me!"

Axreal's eyes resumed blinking normally and her color returned to her skin. She did not seem as frozen as before.

Jerish spoke, "Great! You are coming out of it, Axreal. I am here. Good, you are almost back!"

Axreal's body returned to normal function.

She took in a deep breath. Hunching over, she placed her hands over her knees, exhausted. Then she rose back up and replied, "Oh, Jerish— thank you, Jerish. It was awful. It tried to take me!"

"You're fine now, Axreal. It's over." Jerish rested his arm around her shoulders and continued speaking, "It lost. Come now, we have got to get out of here!"

The System, realizing its own defeat, set about to devise other traps for Jerish and Axreal. Also, The System had yet to determine the unknown's whereabouts within Plantech 3.

Axreal spoke to Jerish despite the overwhelming pain in her head. "I am sure the lab is just beyond that wall. Once there we might be somewhat safer from attacks,"

Both made a breach safely beyond the divide and into the Remoran lab. The room they had entered was dark except for many conduits carrying blue energy and a wide array of machinery lights. Numerous opened podules lined one side.

Watching from behind a girder, Axreal and Jerish saw the first Remoran technician. Its spongy hands reached out from its oddly laid-out body. Where most beings in the Serendipity had symmetry to their design, Remoran bodies had no matching proportions. This had the effect of making them appear strikingly odd, cumbersome, and awkwardly put together. Despite their irregularities, they could move easily and were in fact quite agile. However, no two were ever alike.

One of the technician's eyes was larger than the other. The large eye traveled all about his head on a curving track. With it, he could see all around him and far away. The smaller eye rolled about, confined to a small circular area in the lower right portion of his head. It could see small details, even microscopic ones. The larger eye almost caught sight of the two Setiacotion visitors.

The technician held a seemingly heavy mechanical device, which it rested on a stand. The honeycomb-like device had an oval shape and was overlaid with an alloy mesh. The device expanded and contracted as if it were a balloon repeatedly filling and emptying with air.

"What do you suppose that is?" asked Axreal.

"Whul, I don't know. But did you get a look at that eye?" returned Jerish.

"That is not all that is strange about it. I thought Torbot looked unusual. Remorans are by far the strangest beings we have ever seen," responded Axreal.

"Some of the life forms in the quarries were strange too, but I agree, we've never seen anything like these before," said Jerish.

Axreal and Jerish watched as two others joined the first technician. They opened the closest podule and brought out a Setiacotion female on some sort of stretcher. They kept her unconscious as they moved her into a glass enclosure.

With all three Remorans and the Setiacotion female relocated to the enclosure, Axreal and Jerish felt it was safe to move closer. They peered in and witnessed in disgust the technicians implanting the device into the female's body cavity.

"They must be trying to save her, with the device. Maybe it is some sort of lung. She probably has the 'sickness,'" Axreal said.

"I think you are right. Look here comes another Remoran," spoke Jerish.

"I wonder if that isn't Etrabell. It could be. He seems to be the one in charge," said Axreal.

The Setiacotion female's body twitched back and forth, as they tried to get it to accept the new organ. Axreal and Jerish watched in rapt attention until Axreal took her eyes from the scene to place them studying about the room.

Axreal whispered. "Jerish."

"What is it Axreal?"

"That is my old podule."

"Whul, how do you know?" asked Jerish.

"I have seen it enough times from the outside to know that one used to be mine," said Axreal. "They must have outfitted someone else with it."

"Wait a moment. Where are you going?" asked Jerish.

"I am going to look inside and find out for sure," said Axreal.

"Whul, why is that important?"

"I am curious, that's all," said Axreal, "Stay there and keep watch. The podules are in inactive mode. I'll be safe."

Axreal crawled quickly over to the podule's entry port. She stood up fast and positioned her body sideways. Given her new height, this was an even more difficult task. She had to bend her head back behind her neck as far as she could to be able to make it fit within the contours. She began shuffling her feet side to side while making her way upward towards the main compartment.

Axreal reached her goal; she pried loose, for the last time, the wall segment to her hiding place. Sure enough, her crude foam, lint, and fiber doll sat awaiting rescue.

"Come, we are leaving. We have a much better place to go to. You will never have to be here again," Axreal tucked the doll into her pants pocket, where it would have to ride out the rest of their escape.

Jerish remarked as Axreal crawled back towards him, "Good. You are back."

"What has been going on?" she asked.

"The Remoran in charge is finishing the operation. The other three have moved into another enclosure down there. There has been no sign of The System being alerted to our location yet. I say we move in for a closer look," Jerish said.

They proceeded along the lab's shiny black floor until they got close to the enclosure. They got close enough that they could hear the voice of the one in charge, Etrabell.

Etrabell spoke alone to the semiconscious Setiacotion slave girl. He paused between every sound, making for broken speech. ". . . and with your new breathing organ you'll be able to enter areas of volatile gasses to perform your work and not get sick. Shortly, we can return you to duty, better than before. Here, this will not hurt too much. I am closing up your chest now."

"I am going to talk to Etrabell," said Axreal.

"We don't know what he'll do. Let's go in together," Jerish convinced her.

They entered the enclosure, much to Etrabell's astonishment.

"What!" the Remoran engineer uttered, "Where did you two come from?" He was shocked by their appearances. *They are some other kind of Setiacotion.*

"I am Axreal; this is Jerish, we . . ."

"I must alert The System, you do not belong here. How did you get in here?" he asked.

"NO! Please," Axreal said, "Listen to what we have to say first."

"It is not possible for you to be here. Functioning Setiacotions are confined to the processing areas." Etrabell's torso normally hung weighted to one side. His limbs moved disjointedly as he spoke. "I must continue my work without interruption or there will be punishment."

Jerish jumped in. "Listen, we have been through a lot to get here. The least you can do is hear what we have to say! Then do whatever you must."

Etrabell conceded to Jerish's plea and listened as Axreal spoke. "You once created a retractable arm for me, saving my existence. We are here to save the lives of others. You once told me that you did whatever you could to prevent The System from having us disposed of. Isn't that right?"

"Yes," Etrabell's words gurgled and vibrated out, "but these are the injured. You both do not appear injured, and your presence here is dangerous and will incite The System to come here. There is nothing I can do for you."

"We are not the ones in need of help." Pointing, Jerish said, "We are here to take them to a better place and are seeking your assistance."

"He is right. We are not here for ourselves. We can choose to leave here at any moment. We have come to free as many as we can. We have a vessel waiting to take them out in. We are counting on you to know of a way to transport them through the processing facilities so that we can fly them out."

"I know of no way to do that. Where could you possibly be taking them to, anyways?" Etrabell uttered emphasizing each word. "The injured come here and leave by way of their podules. The only time they do not is when they are sent for disposal. The ones . . . Excuse me just a moment." Etrabell sealed the door closed, which indicated to the other technicians that he did not wish to be disturbed. "The ones that we can't improve upon are exterminated like the rest. We are instructed to place them in there." He pointed out from the windows of the enclosure to an opening. "We inject a chemical that keeps them from moving. Then they are vacuumed into that shoot."

The sight of the chute caused Axreal distress; however, she realized to herself, *It may just be what we are looking for.* "Where does that lead?" she asked.

Etrabell replied, "I have no idea."

Axreal turned to Jerish. "One of us needs to take a look!"

"I will go," said Jerish. "You don't want to see what is in there. I will deal with what I find."

"Are you sure?"

"Yes I am sure. This may be the only way," Jerish said.

With that said, Jerish breached along the chute. Jerish saw where it met up with others. He followed outside along them, coming out temporarily from the breach to gather their location and direction. He followed them, until he came to where they emptied out on Eclipsia's surface.

"This is almost as horrible as the Bereavement Ravine!" Jerish said aloud to himself.

From atop one of the chute's endings, Jerish perched above a horrific sight. At some distance away from Plantech 3, the chutes ended at a two-hundred-foot drop into an enormous pit. The System eventually disposed of all the Setiacotions and Remorans here. The open grave held the corpses of millions.

Jerish held his hands up over his eyes in terror and sadness. At a time like this, it would have been better for Jerish to not have been able to feel his heart. "Axreal should not have to see this! If this is the only way to save them, then we must go through this."

Jerish breached back to the laboratory.

"Axreal, it is a long way, but the chute empties out with others into a massive grave out on the surface. I am thinking one of us can go back and get Torbot and the ACS and pick them up from there."

"Surface—what do you mean?" replied Etrabell. His very large, spongy left hand bounced palm upright as he sought an answer from her.

Axreal looked at Etrabell; her head had to turn up and down to look into both of his eyes. "We need you to load the healed into the chute instead. Can any of the injured be made to last, say, for just a short interval?" Axreal asked.

"Why would we load the repaired to be disposed of? And yes, for some of the Setiacotions we can stop their bleeding and bandage them. But why?" spoke Etrabell.

"Jerish, you breach back and get the ACS and wait at the chute's ending. I will stay here with Etrabell, and when we know you are ready, we can send the escapees through. And get them onboard the vessel."

"I demand to know where you are taking them and what you are doing with them!" spoke Etrabell.

"We haven't the time to fully explain. There is more to existence than The System. They will get the chance to have healthier happier lives," responded Axreal. "Now will you help us or not?"

"If it means they will have a better existence, then I will help. The others must not know what we are up to. I am in charge here, and they are under my authority. However, they are more heavily programmed by The System. They will alert it and, at the very least, not allow us to go against procedure."

"Thank you! Etrabell, I knew you would do the right thing!" Axreal reached out to hug the Remoran. Her arms had a difficult time getting around him though. She also could not get around what appeared to be his confounded look at her.

Then Jerish spoke. "Yes, thank you Etrabell. Axreal, remain safe if anything happens when I breach out of here. I am on my way now. I hope Torbot is okay!"

Jerish managed to breach out of Etrabell's view, going through the multiple walls of the Remoran laboratories to the conveyers. However, he noticed that this time they were empty. Not a single product package in sight. *Why would production stop?* He found this to be very odd. Then he breached up towards the generator's turbine. From there he made his way safely to the landing pad, but nowhere to be seen was the ACS or Torbot.

Inside the lab, Etrabell spoke to Axreal, "I will go and make sure the other technicians are significantly occupied. We have a number of procedures going on right now. There are five Setiacotions, including the one I call Myriel, which you see here in recovery. Later I will have to convince the technicians that these particular operations were not successful and that disposal was called for. We have one other Setiacotion in an intermittent stage. Perhaps I can bandage him well enough for travel. His wounds can't remain unattended for more than a few hours. And, will you please take my lab attendant? He is also in recovery. He is not functioning well here and in fact is prone to accidents. This latest one nearly killed him. Perhaps he will have a chance at a better life with you."

"Sure, that will be fine."

Axreal sunk in utter dismay. *That is only seven we will be able to rescue.* "For a start, that is good. How soon will more arrive at the lab?"

"They come in all the time," Etrabell uttered. "Most will not be in any condition to leave, and it takes awhile to design remedies and improvements for their conditions. Requisitions need to be . . ."

Axreal determined, "We will have to make future trips. We will just have to wait until the technicians make enhancements to the next arrivals."

"Myriel is coming around. I can give her Etazine. It will only keep her out for a short while. She was carrying out her programming when she came in. She'll still try to act it out. When the Etazine wears off you will need to be prepared. She'll not be her normal self until her programming has run its full course."

"Perhaps Jerish and I can come up with a way to keep her safe and secure," said Axreal.

"That would be wise. You will not want her to hurt you or herself during that time. Keeping her safe and secured would only be needed until her programming finishes," spoke Etrabell. "Giving more Etazine to her will only delay her recovery. Then it is up to you."

"I understand. We will eventually have others to help take care of her.

Eventually she'll be like us: healthier, whole, and her own person."

Slowly, ghostlike images of Jerish began to appear. They grew more and more apparent and appeared to coalesce. From them his full living body emerged and he came out of the breach to stand before Axreal and Etrabell.

"OOOHHH," Etrabell stuttered in fright. "How do you accomplish that?"

"It is an ability we have obtained to transport ourselves," replied Jerish. "Whew, it sure takes a lot out of you, though," Jerish paused then spoke, "Axreal?"

"Yes, Jerish."

"I was unable to find Torbot or the ACS. I don't want to think the worst, but I think The System had set a trap for us there, which we were fortunate enough to miss. I hope Torbot found a way to survive."

"I hope so too. But now we need to get Myriel and the other six loaded into the chute," spoke Axreal.

Etrabell had gone about making bandages for the Setiacotion male that as of yet hadn't received his enhancements. Etrabell kept the three other Remoran Lab technicians intensely involved conducting another operation. They would be unable to leave their posts for some time.

He then spoke, "Now I will need your help getting her onto the stretcher. The chute will take her from there. Then we must go and get the other Setiacotions. They did not come in enacting heavy programming, but a little Etazine will keep them sedated and manageable for a while. The bandaged one will need to be moved carefully. My assistant is in another section of the lab. We will have to sneak in and get him out."

"What are we going to do with them outside without the ACS?" Jerish asked, his thick brown brows squeezing together in concern.

"We need to start getting them out now!" spoke Axreal.

Jerish caught a glimpse of something slipping from out of her pants-leg pocket. From what he could see, it did not resemble anything. *How odd. What is Axreal carrying around? A wad of lint? I will have to ask her about that.*

"Jerish, we have got to have a ship!"

"I will somehow find us another one!"

Axreal had an idea. She gave him directions.

Jerish followed them and went off in search of another ACS.

Meanwhile, Axreal made sure that Etrabell did not administer the chemical he was always instructed to inject into those entering the disposal chute. Then she and Etrabell loaded the first six fortunate Setiacotions. However, getting to Etrabell's assistant proved to be much more difficult.

"Axreal I require your assistance to free my attendant."

"What do you need me to do?"

"I will need you to help me load him. He is not yet able to walk. We need to hide him in a service cart. I will be right back with one. Stay here." Etrabell soon returned rolling the service cart. It had two large compartments with sliding doors. Then he said, "Hide inside until we get to the other lab section."

Axreal, reluctant to be confined again, did however get aboard quickly.

When they arrived Etrabell slid open the cart's door. Axreal got out. The lab attendant appeared shocked at the sight of Axreal. Etrabell spoke to him: "Kurby, you get to leave."

Kurby uttered in the usual Remoran fashion, "Where to? Do I have to suit up?"

"No, Kurby, not this time. You won't need your suit any longer."

"I won't need my suit!"

"You are leaving the lab, for good."

Kurby brought his eyes together and replied, "I am? I have been waiting my whole life for this."

"This is Axreal. She knows of a better place. The others can't see you leave. We are going to place you in here, so remain quiet. Axreal grab him here and I will lift him from this side."

Once Kurby was loaded, Axreal hid back inside the service cart. Etrabell managed to drive the cart safely passed several wandering eyes to the disposal chute.

"Axreal, let's load Kurby with the others."

"You are putting me in the disposal chute?" asked Kurby, peering from the cart.

"Quiet Kurby. Not so loud. You won't be harmed," said Etrabell.

"It is how we are going to transport you to safety," Axreal tried to assure him. "Please do not be afraid."

Kurby remained hesitant. Since it meant a chance for something better, he tried not to resist. Besides, he was in no shape to argue.

After they loaded Kurby, Axreal spoke. "I will go ahead and see if Jerish was successful. Don't send them until I return." Then Axreal breached.

Axreal luckily found Jerish waiting. And much to her relief, he had Torbot with him aboard their replacement vessel.

"I am so glad to see you both!" Axreal said.

Jerish spoke. "I did find where The System keeps many ACSs and I . . ."

Axreal interrupted, "I want to hear all about it, but we have six Setiacotions and one Remoran waiting in the chute. Etrabell is guarding them. I need to breach back. We can't keep them waiting. You need to be ready. Remember we have one in bandages and Myriel coming. We also have the Remoran to look out for; he is not able to walk yet."

"Torbot and I will be ready," spoke Jerish.

Axreal left and then reentered the lab.

Axreal spoke to Etrabell, "All right, you can go ahead and turn on the chute. They will all be better once they are freed from here. After we take them where they need to go, Jerish and I will come back for more."

"Thank you Axreal. Someday, I would like to see this 'better place' for myself. I must continue here for now," spoke Etrabell.

He entered a sequence of codes and turned on the chute. Its suctioning increased loudly until it grew almost deafening. It sucked up all seven, delivering them towards their freedom.

Axreal then vanished.

Etrabell called out after their wake, "Farewell, Axreal and Jerish. Good luck, Myriel. Good luck in your new life, Kurby, I will miss you. May you all have good fortune."

Jerish had positioned the ACS so that the disposal chute emptied into the vessel instead of the massive grave. Axreal breached aboard. After a short while, the rescued began to appear one by one and emptied into the ACS. When Myriel arrived, Jerish, Axreal, and Torbot secured her with fasteners that Jerish and Torbot had found earlier in the ACS's hold. They had also made a safe place for the bandaged male to lie down. When Kurby came out from the chute, it took all of Axreal's and Jerish's strength to move him into a room that had space for him. Then they directed the ACS to start flying to make their rendezvous at the quarries.

Meanwhile within the lab, Etrabell slowly walked back to rejoin the other Remoran technicians. He had to come up with a way to acceptably describe to them why so many enhancements did not succeed all at once, and then he would need an acceptable explanation for why Kurby also did not survive.

The System had exhausted all its abilities to recapture and kill the malformations and the unknown in Plantech 3. So it collected its records and compressed itself into data files. The data files converted into microwave signals and were transmitted to the central control hub. The System made for its own escape! And it dutifully notified CreXan!

Then it occurred. A blast like none other. It furiously roared from somewhere centered within Plantech 3. The processing facility shook and filled with pressure and horrific screeching. Despite their message traveling far beyond their confines, millions of screams fell mostly on deaf ears. Matter shook violently. Time and space tore apart. Existence went in and out of phase.

Etrabell did not see it coming. Within seconds, the lab turned into a pressure cooker. The blue energy conduits ruptured and tossed about. The enclosure's glass walls broke and flew off in every direction. The podules rolled about the entire lab like gigantic marbles set loose. The shiny black flooring now became the ceiling. Girders snapped under the shifting weights as everything turned over on itself. One second the lab was there, the next it was completely gone.

The vast, white-hot explosion incinerated the entire processing facility. The massive pressure formed an immense crater underneath. Debris collected in a ring around the smoke-and gas-filled epicenter of the blast.

Shockwaves sent the ACS flying, and the precious few survivors shook aboard.

"Everybody hold on. We are in for a rough ride," spoke Jerish. Axreal, Torbot, Kurby, and the bandaged Setiacotion heard and understood Jerish's words. The five others remained sedated under the effects of Etazine.

"Axreal, hit the throttle and keep an eye out for where we are going," Jerish said.

Notice, there is a large amount of light outside. Gas and debris are coming up from behind the vessel. It appears there has been an explosion at the oviums, Torbot imparted to all.

"Ooohhh," grumbled Myriel, from back within the hold.

"Here, Axreal, I will take over," said Jerish as he grasped the throttle. Outside the explosion subsided and the vessel rumbled to lesser degrees. "You should see what is going on with Myriel," he added.

Axreal rushed to Myriel's side and attempted to calm her. She gently tried to assist the fasteners in keeping Myriel's arms at her sides. A small linear blood stain soaked through Myriel's microfiber work fatigues. It formed from where her incision had yet to heal.

"You will be alright. You do not need to carry out your programming!" Axreal spoke to Myriel, as her body attempted to shuffle during all the ensuing excitement. "We are friends, here to take you to a place where you can get well."

Myriel continued to toss, and the fasteners kept her in place.

Axreal went back up front. While holding onto the instrumentation, she spoke to Jerish, "She hasn't come all the way out yet. I'll keep an eye on her, though."

"That would be best. Torbot, look in on our Remoran friend," said Jerish.

Jerish continued to drive the ACS so that it would keep ahead of the now dissipating shockwave.

Axreal returned to Myriel. Myriel began to grow frantic. Her eyes opened and she jerked about in the programmed motions given to her by The System. Her fingers entered a rhythm of pinching and twisting as if grasping components and they went about in a detailed orchestration. Her legs remained stationary, so it must have been that she was supposed to have been seated at her workstation. She tossed about for a long time until she began to come out from under the programming. She settled down enough for Axreal to take a break and she rejoined Jerish at the controls.

Torbot, out of curiosity, took a quick look at the others. The bandaged male seemed okay, the other four slept despite the turbulence. Afterwards, Torbot looked in on the Remoran. After observing him, Torbot turned to go back up front to join Jerish. That is when Kurby caught sight of the gel creature's glowing body and outstretched arms.

"Hey, don't go. Who are you?" Kurby uttered.

Torbot paused, then instilled into the Remoran's mind, *Greetings. I am Torbot. Jerish, Axreal, and I are taking you to visit my people at one of their colonies. They will try to help you get well. We will also try to help you acclimate to life on the surface of your home world. If you were able to walk, you could come up front to get a look outside at it.*

"I can try to walk now," Kurby said anxiously. Though he could now stand, it would be awhile before he could move normally.

Listen, stay here. I will be back later to check on you. Be careful. Don't try to walk too much, instilled Torbot.

Torbot then went up front and rejoined his comrades. With the majority of their passengers resting or occupied, Jerish, Axreal, and Torbot had some time alone.

"It will be awhile before we locate the colonies," replied Jerish.

"Tell me, how did you find Torbot?" asked Axreal.

Jerish responded, "Whul, like I said before, I encountered a fleet of ACSs. I drove this one out, and then I flew about in search of the disposal chutes' endings and the graveyard. Along the way I saw a place where the used-up ships are disposed of as well. I came across the one we had, and I found Torbot aboard, and scared. As you have noticed, he went through a lot. He told me how he got caught in a trap that had been set for all of us."

"I am grateful you are with us, Torbot!" Axreal said to him.

Certainly, I am also glad to be back amongst friends.

Torbot continued to help direct their way to the quarries while Jerish controlled the vessel.

For all the time Axreal and Jerish had been rescuing the Setiacotions and Remoran out of Etrabell's lab, CreXan had been most splendidly enjoying himself aboard the orbiting Resort Haven. Risase had sensuously approached CreXan with great news.

"Wonderful Supreme Master, it has arrived. They are here!"

She excitedly presented a large, red-foiled package that she clumsily strained to hold up towards him. She caught her heel on the fringe of a plush rug, nearly falling and dropping the package. The contents moved about and the weight shifted inside the box, making her task of holding onto it almost impossible.

CreXan, screamed and blasted, "CAREFUL, they must be in their best condition!"

Risase managed to set the package down in front of CreXan's lower three thumping appendages. While lifting her head, she stopped on her way up. She stared, sidetracked as if lost, into his transparent skin. Perhaps she was mesmerized by the strange patterns the arteries and inner liquids made as they formed and gurgled beneath. Then she shut her eyes and fell in supplication. She laid upon the suite's floor, face down with her arms stretched wide in reverence to her master.

"Forgive me Majesty, for you deserve much better than I. I will be more careful."

"You may rise," CreXan ordered.

Risase stood with her head hung low.

CreXan released his condescending slitted eyes from their disdain and opened them with an equal amount of excitement. Then he swallowed a large savoring of Citmop. This particular platter had three levels so that flavorings dripped from above to land below where they added a little something extra.

Risase spoke, "More pleasure awaits you, O Wonderful CreXan!"

"Come, my pretty Kanda drudge. What have you in store for me?"

"Surprises for His Greatness await in the Grand Arena."

"Accompany me," CreXan ordered Risase.

CreXan slithered up onto his resort skid. Risase had the extreme pleasure of CreXan allowing her to ride the skid. Lorese had always been made to walk everywhere. Risase sat proudly with CreXan's package in the back of the skid. They rode down the numerous gaudy corridors leading to the Grand Arena.

Once there, four male Kanda carried their master to his front row throne. Risase then handed the shiny package to one of them and he quickly left with it. After a glimpse of himself in his mirror CreXan remarked to himself, "How exquisite." He inhaled a wisp of the swirling, perfumed incense that fragranced the arena.

Next, the drudges presented him with a glass, gold, and bejeweled chalice. It had a loop in its handle designed for each of his talons. CreXan took a walloping gulp of its intoxicating punch, its froth spilled over as the arena's curtains parted.

Risase could not contain her excitement any longer and she began fiercely applauding, so much so that her hands hurt. She found her actions to be true to herself. She would never understand that The System had programmed her to believe and act in certain ways. Her personality had been a creation of The System. The true person had never been able to form on its own.

With the curtains parted, CreXan looked into the arena below. A concealed container held something in the center. A heavily pocked and very tall Kanda brought the package and released its contents into the ring. All around the arena torches added dramatic effect to the spectacles performed there.

CreXan raised his talons into the air in approval as the contents spilled out of the foil wrapping. Two round creatures, resembling a cross between a gourd covered in warts and a bird, tumbled out and began a mad dash around the inside of the ring. The Chicgeza were nearly flightless fowl, indigenous to Preadues, a planet within the consumer-world territories. Preadues contained mainly lower-brain carriers and was of little use to anyone, except for the Lam Warons enjoying the strange mating instincts of its chief bird. They also made a delicious meal.

The Kanda attendants lifted the veil from the container in the center of the ring. Within it sat motionless a fat Chicgeza female. She looked dumbstruck through the glass container as the two male Chicgeza outside began to fight each other in an attempt to win her as a mate. Her pheromones made their way through holes in the container's wall. Her iridescent colorings further enticed her would-be suitors. It was the mating season. And the males naturally fought to the death. The two males crazily ran about picking at each other, until the weaker fell in pain and exhaustion.

CreXan enjoyed the spectacle, so much so that he had a difficult time keeping his body arched to remain seated the whole time.

"Wonderful. More! I must have more!"

The curtains closed and then reopened for act two. Two Kandas entered from opposite sides of the high-ceilinged arena and they descended the steps to the wrestling mat below. They approached each other ready to wrestle, as CreXan made a mental wager on which one he thought would win.

"Risase, who do you think will triumph?" CreXan turned towards his chief Kanda drudge.

"O Your Magnificence, only you will triumph," she spoke.

"Alas, I will inherit my rightful standing. You are so right. But I mean between them."

"O Your Grace, I have to say that, that one seems stronger and more likely to win," Risase pointed towards the larger of the two.

He had well-developed muscles for a Kanda. Most likely he had trained his whole existence just for this particular performance.

The Kanda wrestlers wore form-fitting garments about their waists. Both drew their arms and lunged at each other. The larger bounced on his knees and the smaller, more youthful one danced around the arena to avoid his opponent. After much tumbling, lunging, strangling, sweat, and flying, the larger Kanda snapped the smaller one's neck. He bowed, victorious, to CreXan as the second act concluded.

"Splendid! Risase, you were right! More!"

The floor holding Risase and CreXan within his chair rotated, leaving the arena to face another ornately curtained stage.

Unexpectedly, the miniature portable interface blinked and called for CreXan's attention. The voice of The System spoke. "Unable to apprehend escaped Setiacotions. All means exhausted. Plantech Processing Facility 3 has been destroyed."

"Eeeehhh. Can you positively confirm that the malformations are finally dead?" CreXan demanded to know.

"Positive confirmation can't be established. Escape is probable."

"If those malformations somehow managed to survive, they may show up again! You are not to allow them entrance! I command you to place all processing facilities on alert. I wanted Obscuria to have been ready yesterday. I need to move. I need the new manufacturing world to take over full and complete operations, NOW! Eeehhh, then it won't matter about the Setiacotions, or Eclipsia, or any malformations. We can blow the whole place up and be done with it!"

The System responded, "Impenetrable wall barrier enhanced at all Eclipsian processing facilities. Quantum molecular array now in place. Obscuria is sixty-five percent operable. Full integration of the harvested species is complete. Processing facilities under further construction. Full operation in fifteen intervals possible."

"I can't wait that long! I want it done in seven. Or I will get myself a whole new operating system! What use is a system that can't serve me right! I shouldn't have to do anything for myself! I surely shouldn't have to do all your thinking! AAAGGHH. Inform me right away if there are any attempts to enter the processing facilities by anyone from outside The System! Is that clear?"

"Information received."

The miniature interface's holographic display faded and CreXan gathered a less tense composure. Exhaling through his fangs, he let out a high-pitched, shrill sigh. *The System has failed me, over and over again, against those malformations! It is leaving me no other choice.* CreXan realized what was becoming necessary.

Now, with immediate business taken care of, he wanted to get back to enjoying himself. He tried to reposition his segmented bulk within his throne.

"Refill my chalice and prop me up!"

The stage curtains parted to present him with act three. The stage held a large, three-level transparent obstacle course. At previous performances, when released into the structure, sometimes chased and sometimes alone, the Kanda and the Chicgeza made their way to the exit. The obstacle course had some walls that could not be seen, only felt. It also had sloping stairs, opening and closing doors, twists and turns, mirrors, pitfalls, sharp edges, and difficult-to-maneuver mazes. At one point inside, there was an antigravity chamber that the occupant had to move between. The occupant would also have to walk narrow ledges, grab hold of ceiling bars to pull himself forward, and walk across rotating and spinning paths.

CreXan had a splendid idea, "Risase, how would you like to enter the obstacle course?"

"Could I really, O Great and Supreme Majesty? It would be such an honor," Risase replied.

"Yes! By all means enter!" squealed CreXan.

Risase entered the first floor and went about in confusion. However, she was motivated to do her best as her master's slitted eyes were upon her. Her head slammed into the unseen walls a few times. Once to CreXan's deep satisfaction, Risase bent over pressing her rear flat against the glass. Her idiotic display kept CreXan laughing; he almost brought up his Citmop at the hilarious performance Risase put on. Risase was determined, despite lacking enough common sense to get through the obstacle course quickly. At one point she slid on Chicgeza feathers and droppings and began to itch uncontrollably. Obviously, the Kanda had not cleaned up very well after the last time the course was used. She scratched crazily as she made her way through the obstacles, which amused CreXan all the more. The exit appeared right in front of her, then she stopped, hesitated, and decided to turn around, and she headed the other way.

"Could you be any more stupid?" shrieked CreXan.

The obstacle course shielded Risase from hearing CreXan's insults.

Risase's performance lasted so long that the Kanda arena attendants had to cut her out and rescue her from the obstacle course. The Kanda freed her, and she rejoined CreXan at his throne.

With the show over, matters pressed upon CreXan once again and he became serious. He shouted while addressing Risase, as his face muscles tightened, "The System is leaving me no choice. I am going to have to make sure those malformations didn't survive. And if they did, I will have to take care of them the old-fashioned way! For that, all I will need is a little research and I should be able to do it!"

"What, Your Greatness, do you mean?" spoke Risase as she stood by. "Your loyal Kanda and servants will do whatever you ask. Do not trouble yourself so. There isn't anything we won't do for you. All will be done for you."

"NO, Risase. The only way it will get done right is if I do something about this myself." CreXan's nodules seemed to want to burst with all of his frustration. His chelatenous outer coating seemed to weigh more of late. He continued by ordering, "Have *The Alustria* prepared for my departure! I want it loaded with a supply of Caselsalt gas. If I discover the malformations, Caselsalt gas should be effective in rendering them susceptible to me. I need to look some things up first. Then I am going down to the surface myself. I will make sure those malformations did not survive!"

"Majesty, do you wish for me to accompany you?"

"NO! You stay here!"

"I will pack your Chicgeza salad for your trip. How much would you like?"

"Chop up all of them!"

Once ready, *The Alustria*, under CreXan's verbal commands, launched. It would take some time before it could reach the planet's surface, as the Resort Haven orbited at quite some distance. He would have the full vessel flown down below to begin his search.

Auria Isis

For Axreal, Jerish, Torbot, and their band of survivors, the situation aboard the automatic control ship had grown somewhat calmer. They had gotten closer to the quarries when all of the sudden a single sphere of light entered through the viewport.

The light sphere met up with Jerish, Axreal, and Torbot. Spinning all about the two Setiacotions and their gel friend, in chiming radiance, the astral melody poured forth:

For so long have I waited; all can be as it once was. Far and beyond, wondrous realities lay ahead for you, and for all. Imagine wholeness. You can achieve more than you can possibly know. All is within your grasp, all can be as it was meant. Freedom, joy, and harmony can return. For more of my children are set free and returning . . .

"Axreal! It's *her*. It is the song," exclaimed Jerish. The swelling sensation in his now matured and expanding heart drove him to tears. The song resonated within him and it was beautiful and soothing.

"I know, I hear it too." Axreal felt warmth, relaxation, and joy overtake her.

The astral melody also played within Torbot's mind to his equally ecstatic response. All of his gel arms extended, tripling his size. With a gleeful squeak, bubbles began to float from his mouth. This showed a gel creature at his happiest.

From within the light came a crisp voice, "Children, I am Auria Isis. That is the name my children once called me, my forgotten name. I am the spirit of your world. I have been with you, encouraging you. It was I who helped send powers to awaken abilities within you for your escape. I could do this because, Axreal and Jerish, you were the most receptive to them and the most in need. By way of your seizures, Axreal, and by way of your tantrums, Jerish, I was able to help in freeing you both. They allowed me the space to come in and help you have the ability to breach. It has been eons since I have taken this form. My spirit dwells with my children, and now resides best in the nearby quarries. Hope abounds. Because you have been freed, all can be as it once was. Your home once supplied your every need. In balance and beauty did we all live. Children, for so very long I have been wounded. I can feel this newest of wounds most horrifically. Still, there is a chance that things can return. The wonderful lives you were meant to have can be again. Full, rewarding, complete lives, and more can be yours. When you live in harmony with me, there are no pains or ills. I have been lost and wounded but now all can be restored."

Axreal and Jerish, with Torbot clinging between them, wept profoundly, knowing that the spirit of their world had taken rare form to grace them with her very presence. Their mother had spoken to them!

"We are deeply thankful to you," spoke Axreal and Jerish together.

We are grateful beyond measure, imparted Torbot. *Your presence honors the past, present and future!*

"You are welcome, dear ones. However I cannot remain long. I have even more to mourn for now. But children, I am most proud of what you have done. There is still much more ahead for you. Love one another and live more like Torbot's people do. In such can you find happiness, peace, harmony, and support. Look out for all living things. Dignity is only the beginning. There is more than you can possibly know, wondrous realities lay ahead for you."

Eclipsia, Auria Isis as she was properly called, formed into beam of light, flew backwards out the viewport, and appeared to ascend back into the moon. She had vanished. The vessel reappeared to Jerish, Axreal, and Torbot. They watched through the viewport as the first quarry came into view.

"That was amazing!" said Jerish while facing Axreal. "She helped us to get free and has been encouraging us all along."

"She wants things to be like they once were, before the Lam Warons ruined everything!" spoke Axreal.

Be aware, Torbot redirected their attention to the quarries outside. *I will need to inform them of what has happened. No doubt they will be concerned, because they will have felt the effects of the shockwave and maybe have seen the explosion.*

"You are right. While you inform your people, Jerish and I can tend to the others," said Axreal.

Jerish, this is a good place to land, Torbot motioned to a level space close to the rooftop membrane of a very large quarry.

Jerish set the ACS down.

Shortly, I will be back, Torbot sprang from the woven hatch.

"I wonder how they are doing?" asked Axreal.

Axreal and Jerish checked in on their passengers. Myriel seemed afraid, but fortunately her System programming had worn off. Kurby's ability to walk had returned. The four sedated Setiacotions had recovered from the effects of Etazine and sat confounded. They had no idea where they were or what was going on.

Jerish spoke, "What about him?" He nodded in the direction of the bandaged male. "He isn't looking so well now."

"We need to get him out first. Let's get everyone together. Myriel can be unfastened now. Let's bring her, Kurby, and the other four in here so we can explain what has happened and what we are planning on doing. Later Torbot will come back and we can all get underway."

With the rescued gathered in the hold with the bandaged male, Jerish addressed the group.

"I know," spoke Jerish confidently, "that you all are scared and don't know about everything that is going on. Axreal and I have helped bring you to the outside. You are no longer in the processing facilities nor a part of The System. We are aboard a vessel that has landed on the outside. After a while we are going to take you to some people that will care for you and give you nourishment and rest. You will be safe with them." Glancing more specifically at the bandaged male, Jerish continued, "They will also tend to your wounds." Then he continued speaking with emphasis to all of the group. "After you are rested, for the Setiacotians, the gel creatures will help you through a process. If you notice, Axreal and I are like you but also more vital, healthy, and strong. Whul, that is because we have already undergone the changes. You will also undergo similar changes for your well-being." Then he took notice of the Remoran assistant's enthusiasm. "Kurby?"

Kurby uttered in excitement, "When can I start my new life at the 'better place' Etrabell told me about?" He brought both eyes forward to pay full attention to Jerish's reply.

"Soon, Kurby. Very soon," replied Jerish.

Torbot leapt back aboard, joined by two of his counterparts.

Jerish spoke so that everyone would be made aware. "This is Torbot. He can communicate directly into your mind. It is his people we have come to see. Come everyone, we have something wonderful to show you."

Torbot perched up high so as to address the group, *Be aware. Where we are taking you is a fragile place. Your future lives will depend on nurturing and taking care of it. Please follow closely and pay attention.*

Axreal called to Jerish. Referring to the bandaged male, she spoke, "You and I will need help carrying him down there."

"Hey," Jerish motioned for two of the other Setiacotions, "help us. We have to carefully get him down below first."

The two aided Jerish and Axreal as the gel creatures directed the entire group towards the quarry oasis.

They continued downward. When they came to the end of the descending pathway, Jerish, Axreal, and the others gently set the bandaged male on the ground.

Torbot imparted to all, *Be aware. This is similar to how our world outside once used to be. It is my people's strong desire that you will aid us in starting the process of returning it to the way it once was.*

Torbot, along with many of the gel creatures, began to explain everything to the new arrivals. They would be given rest, suitable natural food, new attire, and have their medical needs tended to. Once situated, the metamorphosis could begin for them!

What being out on the surface of his home world would mean for Kurby remained to be seen. What those changes would be, the gel creatures could only speculate.

Jerish took Axreal aside. "It feels good to be back!"

"I agree," she replied. "What else are you thinking about?"

"Whul, we still haven't found a way to the Haven. I can't just give up."

"We won't. We will just have to wait till an opportunity presents itself, though. We should head for another processing facility and try another rescue, soon," Axreal spoke.

"I am wondering what the metamorphosis will bring for them,

especially Kurby. It might be useful for us to wait awhile and see what happens."

Axreal and Jerish decided to remain for a short time in the safety of the quarries. They concluded that an interval's rest might also do them some good. As they spoke together, off to their side at the quarry wall, numerous gel creatures rolled out from a tunnel from an adjoining quarry. They had come to assist with the new arrivals.

Torbot rejoined Jerish and Axreal, *Stay. You both have been through a lot. With a little rest you can make up your minds about how to proceed. They have told me that Ator has sent word for me. She has a surprise back at the nest. I think since I have been away I have become a father. If I am right, my babies will need my care.*

"That is great news, pal!" spoke Jerish.

"Wonderful, Torbot," said Axreal.

"Then you'll probably want to be returning home soon," said Jerish.

Understand, Torbot imparted, *it has been a grand experience traveling with you both. I must finish inscribing my notations of what took place. Someday other generations will need to read about these events. Along the journey, I helped stop a vile contraption. I found many areas that will provide bountiful gatherings for Evalious Navitilium. I encountered an alien hunter, who also was from beyond our world. I witnessed an ancient transformation. I traveled past the borders of our explored territories and rode on giant machines. I flew above the sky and entered partway into the oviums. I nearly cooked to death and I saw the spirit of my world. I have gathered much in the way of knowledge. It has been an exceptional journey. But yes, Jerish and Axreal, after I finish here in the quarries, I must return home to the nest. My future lies there.*

"Whul, I will be sad to see you leave, pal. Perhaps we can come and visit you again," spoke Jerish. His smoky blue eyes filled with liquid.

Pleasant. Ator would like that very much, I am sure. Many in the colony would be surprised to see you. My people will be here to assist you and the others. There will be much work ahead for you. You must learn how to provide, food, garments, and shelter for yourselves without harming the planet, and to do so in harmony and balance. Never take more than you need. As long as you, the Setiacotions, and Remorans live in harmony with the world, your needs will be provided. Study the ways of my people, they will guide you in how best to survive.

Axreal and Jerish spoke in unison, "In all we do, we will honor your ways."

Axreal spoke, "Torbot, when we first met I was scared by you. But I am grateful you followed along with us. I learned a lot from you. You are a great friend and you will always have a place in my mind and heart."

Jerish, sobbing, said, "I don't want you to go!" When he realized Torbot had no choice, he spoke, "Take care, pal!"

Farewell, Jerish and Axreal.

Jerish could not watch as Torbot collected his carryall, made his last impartations with the colony scientists, and bounced away along the pathway home.

Axreal grasped Jerish's hand and they turned back toward the quarry colony. Axreal spoke. "They are preparing food for us; we should go."

After a well-balanced, healthful meal, Jerish and Axreal got a good night's slumber.

After a good duration, Axreal and Jerish awoke from the sleeping mats the gel creatures had prepared for them. They discovered the living museum about them was bustling with activity. The increase in movement by the Setiacotions and gliding gel creatures broke apart the delicate flyers from their airborne formations. They also noticed the flower buds of Orcadian Huim had tightened and closed, having also turned a reddish purple. The swooping Maxurous Stravous vines lay drooping on the ground. Their season was coming to a close.

Gel creatures had gathered the rescued Setiacotions to prepare them for their new life. The gel creatures cared and tended for them as if they were newly released seedlings. Given enough light, purified water, proper nourishment, and the proper instructions, they would now germinate properly.

With the possibility of more future arrivals, the colony scientists had formulated a plan. They had laid the groundwork so that eventually the returning Setiacotions and Remoran, and any Kanda who might possibly return, would work to help enlarge the quarries. With the added help, the gel creatures could hollow out more living space to accommodate the needs of a growing population.

Myriel, looking like she had just come out from under a terrible gloom, walked up to Axreal. She spoke with a rasp in her voice. "They say we are going to go through a metamorphosis. That most likely the device inserted in me will be completely expelled and I'll be made well. I won't have to make clothes, toys, conductors, utensils, hardware, and all that equipment anymore? I won't have to mix compounds, or measure, or dig, or lift all that junk? And I will be able to breathe correctly? I won't have to labor in those ways anymore! This is because of you and Jerish?"

Axreal pressed her hands down the sides of her golden hair. "Whul," Axreal caught herself sounding like Jerish, "We did what we had to. We could not have done it without the help of Torbot, the gel creatures, and most of all, Auria Isis. Jerish and I still must go back to the processing facilities and try to rescue the rest."

"Who is Auria Isis?" Myriel wanted to know.

"She reached out to Jerish and me in the darkest, most painful point of our existences and helped us escape. She encouraged us along the way, and she revealed to us that she was the spirit of our world. When you are well, perhaps you will hear her sing!"

"I think I would like that."

"Oh, I am sure you would. It is quite beautiful. She wants us to return to the way things were once, before the Lam Warons destroyed most of our world and took us hostage." Axreal noticed some of Torbot's people motioning for Myriel. Axreal spoke, "Looks like they need you. Don't be afraid. Things are going to get a whole lot better for you. Hopefully, we can talk again soon. Here, I want you to take this," Axreal reached into her pants-leg pocket and presented to Myriel her foam, lint, and fiber doll.

Myriel took the doll into her hands saying, "What, is this?"

"I made her so I'd never feel alone. She was there for me when I had no one else. Will you take care of her now?"

"I most certainly will. Thank you, Axreal," Myriel said. Then she rejoined the other Setiacotions.

Surveying the rescued, Axreal remembered, *Seven. We only managed to get seven.*

Next Axreal turned and watched as Jerish splashed his face with purified water in a container the gel creatures had given him.

Jerish set the container down on a grassy spot and approached her. "Let's get back to the vessel and head out for another rescue attempt." He finished pat-drying his face, then he and Axreal made their way to the ACS.

A Merciless Storm

Back in flight, with Eclipsia's molten rock speeding below, Jerish and Axreal set out towards a rather ominous processing facility. Its great dockyards stood more than one-hundred stories above. In compliance with CreXan's demands, preparations for relocation were well underway. Ships were transporting fabrications, supplies, and installations to the new operations on Obscuria. Very shortly, these particular Eclipsian facilities would run their full course. Their exterior connectways coiled like a million snakes piled upon each other. Their pulses of eerie blue energy slowed with the decreasing rate of production.

"What do you suppose that is?" asked Axreal, peering through the viewport.

"I don't know. But we're not going in there . . . I'm going to turn us around."

"Good idea."

Ahead in the distance, low-lying clouds had amassed, consisting of two types of water. One type of cloud appeared iridescent; the other was heavier, oily like, and had an overall transparent green color. When they came in contact with each other, the two types of clouds always made for an abrupt storm. Suddenly, the viewport filled with a huge surge of weather activity, and the storm pulled the ACS in.

"We aren't turning!" yelled Axreal.

"I'm trying! It's not that easy," replied Jerish, clenching his teeth.

The alternating air pressures outside caused the viewport to split and crack like a lightning strike.

"Oh no, Axreal! I don't have control anymore!"

"Just let go. The storm has us! The viewport isn't holding . . . get down!" Axreal screamed.

Just then, hit by a giant splash, the viewport flew apart. The two waters churning in conflict filled the cabin up to the control panel.

Axreal and Jerish emerged drenched and cold. Their recycled cloth garments sagged and weighed them down, making movement even more difficult. They waded in the chaotic mixture trying to find a secure place to hold onto.

"Grab on. Up there, above your head," spoke Jerish.

"It's slippery. I can't," Axreal spoke. Then she noticed something. "Look, it's the fasteners we used to secure Myriel, over there, floating."

Jerish reached out and grasped at them. He tossed one to Axreal and kept one for himself while letting the rest go.

Simultaneously they spoke, "Let's hook them up there!"

They each flung their fasteners around a support beam and held on to both ends to keep themselves secured to the vessel.

Outside, each of the two waters fought to rebond with its own type. As rapidly and violently as they had collided, the waters now separated. They regrouped back into clouds and violently repelled each other, sending each other off in opposite directions. The storm started to dissipate, leaving behind a lifting fog and remnants of foam everywhere.

Without the storm holding it up, the ACS was now freefalling, spiraling out of control. Upon hitting the ground, it was unable to release its legs. It slid across the surface, pushing the fog away. Jerish and Axreal held on for their lives until it came to a stop.

"Whew! It's over. I think we can let go now," spoke Jerish.

"The ship is dead," Axreal noticed.

"Whul, let's get out and see where we are."

With Jerish in the lead and Axreal following, they slushed across the deck plates, kicking up foam as they made their way to the hatch. Jerish opened it, and they stepped outside while sifting through the fog.

"This is different. The ground, it's not the same," said Axreal looking down. Water drained from her nostrils.

Jerish looked ahead from in and out of the moving fog, then whispered, "Axreal, quiet. It's a circle of . . . people. Setiacotions!"

"I see them also. Let's watch for a while."

"Whul, I'm going to go see what they are doing!"

Axreal spoke, "I can't tell if they are doing anything at all. Have you even seen them, *move*?"

"No. Maybe we don't need to worry so much."

Axreal and Jerish proceeded to walk up toward the Setiacotions.

Tranquil, placid faces with slightly arched bodies began to emerge from the fog. There appeared to be six Setiacotions holding hands and standing in a circle with their backs towards a pond. The foam covering them began to dissipate as the temperature rose slightly.

"They aren't even alive," spoke Jerish.

"Do you notice? They have our height." said Axreal. "They are some kind of statues," she said while tracing their contours with her fingers.

As more of the fog lifted, more sights came into view. A cobbled street, with white inlaid, polished stones lay at their feet. Building fronts began jutting out. The lifting fog revealed doorways and oval window openings. Lanterns hung from the roofs and overhead a network of walkways connected the buildings' varying levels. The buildings had smooth, white walls. They curved, reaching upwards in the middle to form an assortment of pointed roofs.

Jerish spoke, raising his brows, "Amazing! This must be a colony of some kind! Look, it extends all around us."

"Do you think this is where our people once lived?" said Axreal.

"It could be!" replied Jerish.

"But how can it be here?"

"Maybe we were taken way off course by the storm," said Jerish.

"That would be the most reasonable explanation," said Axreal. "Also, it seems to be in good condition."

From a building behind them, a window with creaking hinges abruptly slammed shut.

"What?!?" Jerish and Axreal became startled.

They turned, locating where the sound had come from. Their ears directed them to a particular upper level window. They looked up at it. Then they heard sounds coming from within.

"Someone is in there!" said Axreal.

"Let's go find out," said Jerish, rubbing his hands together to create some warmth.

"This leads to an entry close to that window," Axreal said as she pointed out a particular walkway.

Axreal and Jerish clasped hands to help stabilize each other as they made their way up the curving walkway. The walkways had no railings or walls on which to rely.

Upon making it to the odd, oval-shaped entry Axreal remarked, "Now what? Should, we just go in?"

"Perhaps we should say something." said Jerish. Then he leaned inwards so that his voice met the transparent openings of the entry. "Is anyone in there?"

No sound or response came.

"Try using the lever, but do it slowly. Let's see if it opens," remarked Axreal.

Jerish grasped the lever and turned it. Its cold metal-like handle had numerous bumps on it, which made it easier to grip.

"Axreal, it's turning on its own!"

The two of them tilted back on their heels in fright as the entryway opened.

Messellorn opened the front door and rolled up his sleeves. Seeing the two young adults, he spoke, "Yes? May I help you?"

The sight shocked Jerish and Axreal, and they starred dumbfounded, not knowing what to do.

"It's cold out. That was quite some storm we just had. Step inside. We'll get you something warm to drink," spoke Messellorn. He dressed in a very detailed fashion, looking like a business owner.

Jerish and Axreal, hesitantly stepped in.

With Messellorn's back to them, Axreal whispered quickly to Jerish, "This can't be possible. There are no Setiacotions outside."

"Here, sit a moment. I'll have my mate bring you some steamed Orangeous tea. It should take the nip off," Messellorn said while leaving the room.

Jerish and Axreal remained seated on an odd couch, sinking deep into the puffy, purplish seat cushions.

"I don't believe this," spoke Axreal.

"Yeah. I'm getting a strange feeling. But this is real. He is Setiacotion. Whul, I mean, I don't think we are dreaming."

"Maybe we hit our heads during the storm and are knocked out. But then how is it we are talking to each other?"

"No! We are definitely here. Let's just keep going and we'll figure out what is happening. And be careful. Just don't say too much."

"Right. We can't reveal we are suspicious."

Messellorn returned carrying a tray with three tea mugs. "I am called Messellorn by the way. So, are you from Verdex Township? I haven't seen you around. You're not Elix's kids?"

Axreal thought to herself, *This doesn't make any sense. Ruins would be one thing. But an intact town with living people. I hope Jerish knows not to drink any of that.*

"No," replied Jerish.

"You're not from our town, or you're not Elix's kids?" wondered Messellorn.

"Neither," said Jerish quickly, still struck by the odd sights.

"Oh well, doesn't matter. You can stay for a while. Here, drink up."

"Ah," replied Axreal hesitantly.

"She hasn't been feeling well lately," Jerish came to Axreal's aid.

"Here, take it anyways. You might change your mind," said Messellorn to Axreal.

"I'll have some," spoke Jerish. "It might do me some good." He glanced at Axreal from out of Messellorn's view, shaking his head back and forth, to indicate to her that he had no intention of drinking the "Orangeous Tea" either.

"Well, you're from out of the township, then. You must have had a rough ride."

Axreal and Jerish both thought about the ACS. How would it manage to sit out in the plaza and not be brought to anyone's attention?

"Oh, yes. That was some storm," said Axreal.

"Well, you are welcome to relax here. Enjoy yourselves in the company of our home. Your garments will dry faster if I turn up the heat source. I could have my mate bring you some fresh garments. By the way, those are strange ones you've got on."

"Sure, fresh garments would be nice," said Jerish as he nodded to Messellorn, and also to Axreal.

"You will want to stay. Perhaps you'll like it so much, you'll never want to go back to wherever that was you said you were from before. Yes, I insist you stay. Make this your home."

Messellorn got up to speak to his, as of yet unseen, mate, "Dear, see if you can find some of Gleshe's clothes. Our guests need dry garments. They are going to be with us for a while."

Jerish saw his chance and whispered to Axreal, "Maybe we should get out of here."

Jerish motioned for them to get up and try for the entry. They rose up, only to find it locked. Looking through the transparent openings, it appeared that the fog had returned. They hurried to sit back down as Messellorn reentered the room.

"Were you up?" asked Messellorn. "There's no need for that. I'd like you to be comfortable. Forget your worries."

"We don't want to trouble you any. We had not planned on staying. We are just passing through. We need to get going soon," Jerish said.

"Right," replied Axreal. "We will be expected."

"No, that wouldn't be wise. The storm. It has a way of coming back sometimes, before it is completely over. It is dangerous to be out in it. Here, I haven't seen you drink anything yet."

Jerish spoke, "Yeah." He brought the tea up to his lips. The smell of Orcadian Orangeous fruit peels wafted in the air. He did feel hungry for the taste of them. It smelled wonderful. A little sip might not hurt.

Jerish, what are you doing! Axreal thought while nudging Jerish's side to bring back his attention to the fact that it might not be such a good idea. She poked him a couple of times.

Jerish spilled a little of the tea, and a portion ran hot down his stubble-covered chin.

"See, looks like the storm is coming back," Messellorn looked through the window coverings. "The plaza will fill again and no one should be out in that. Here," he reached into a chest and pulled out a type of game. "We can play Rumble. It'll be great fun!"

Messellorn presented the game and set it up on a table before them. It appeared to be carved out of some type of gnarled and polished wood. He explained to Jerish and Axreal how it was to be played. It had numerous levels laid out, much like the walkways outside. At four corners sat the players' pieces. Players took turns rolling dice and moving their characters through the levels to be first to the top. Where you landed determined your next move and whether you got one or not. Some spaces were "Rumbles"—if a player landed on one he would be knocked off by the other players and have to start at the beginning.

"Here," Messellorn handed the dice to Axreal. "You roll to see who goes first."

Somehow Axreal became enthralled by the distractions of the game. She felt compelled to play. Jerish also became mesmerized by the prospect of playing the game.

"Now you roll," Messellorn spoke to Jerish while handing him the dice. Jerish rolled. "Okay, now I will roll. Looks like you go first," he motioned to Jerish. "I warn you. I am impossible to beat."

Jerish, Axreal, and Messellorn took turns playing Rumble. Jerish began to enjoy himself in the comfort and coziness that surrounded them. He had to admit he was having fun. While making one of his moves, he reached for the Orangeous tea and took a sip.

"Good, very good," replied Messellorn. "Your turn," he motioned to Axreal.

Axreal had a nagging sensation tug at her, like a faint whisper in her mind she heard, *Weren't we supposed to be going somewhere? There was something important Jerish and I were doing. Very important . . .*

"Oh, looks like you landed on a Rumble! You'll have to go back to the start," Messellorn told Axreal, as he knocked her piece off the board. She picked it back up, placing it at her starting spot.

"Now it is my turn," Messellorn chuckled.

Jerish watched as his turn would be next. *This can't be right. What are we doing here? This game…it is taking control of us!*

"Here drink some more, that's it," Messellorn told Jerish. "I am your friend. Friends enjoy spending time with each other. I will show you a good time. We will stay here enjoying ourselves," Messellorn then whispered under his breath, "forever."

Axreal rolled the dice and got back into the game.

Messellorn's turn was next. He rolled the dice and landed on a spot that gave him another chance to roll. Rolling again, he entered his piece into the winning circle, "See, I told you I always win! Come now, you both played very well. You even had me going a couple of times. Now it is time to put you both down to sleep. Here, my mate has prepared your hammocks…"

Jerish and Axreal rose up, like puppets on a string.

Messellorn led them to an alcove where their resting places awaited them, "You will be so comfortable in here. No worries. Endless comfort. Endless peace. Endless rest."

I don't want to make myself comfortable. Others need my help. Yeah…there were others that needed me and Axreal. I was going somewhere to help others . . . Jerish thought, then spoke aloud, "Axreal this is all wrong. We can't go in there!"

"I'm trying not to. But somehow it feels good. I know you are right. We have something we are supposed to be doing."

"Silence! I don't want to hear you talking anymore! It is time for sleep…You need your rest, after all!" Messellorn grew agitated.

"Axreal, step back! Whatever he has for us in there is not good!"

Jerish stretched his arm across Axreal's path. She butted up against his sleeve.

Messellorn turned back around to face them. He spoke, "Now, now, I'll hear none of that! What I am offering you both is so much easier. Don't trouble yourselves. With a little nap, you'll never have to worry again, never have to be bothered. You can stop being chased. All your troubles will vanish into thin air!" Messellorn moved to grab Jerish and Axreal to force them to follow.

"I WILL SEE THE TRUTH!" Jerish confidently demanded. With

those powerful words, things began to unravel around them. He made the right choice and his heart was telling him so.

"Eeehhh, you malformations make up your own reality. The truth is that you are going in there whether you like it or not!" Messellorn hissed.

Jerish and Axreal fled with Messellorn chasing them.

"Jerish! Messellorn sounds different. And what is that smell?"

"What smell? There's one coming from the heat source and the tea smells *good*…"

"No! It is something closer to us."

"Yeah, you are right. I notice it now. It's everywhere," he spoke.

"We've gotta get out of here!"

With the powers of his illusions failing to keep a hold on Jerish and Axreal, CreXan was, among other things, failing to keep his odor masked. Lam Warons had a hard time tolerating their own foul smell. Often, other alien races found it impossible to tolerate, unless it was somehow hidden.

CreXan's illusions were coming undone. Jerish and Axreal saw Messellorn's true appearance, that of CreXan. It would take all of CreXan's powers to bring them back under his spell, and he had no more of the Caselsalt with which to make them vulnerable. He had used it all up when he doused them aboard the ACS at the start of the illusion. He felt his ruse coming apart. The strain of maintaining it was weakening him.

"What is that?" asked Axreal.

Jerish saw the ugly creature before them. He had a gut feeling about it.

He realized he did not need to have Marshall's portable device. He knew for a fact what stood before them: "That is a Lam Waron!"

"Ohhh, Jerish!" cried Axreal.

All around Jerish and Axreal, Eclipsia's molten rock began to reappear. Reality had returned, and they were merely outside. There had been no storm, no fountain of people, no Setiacotion village and no Messellorn! Only CreXan, perched in the middle of his web of illusions, like a spider ensnarling its prey.

It had all been an elaborate Lam Waron illusion. It had all been a lie, intended to cause Jerish and Axreal to want to sleep, forever.

Now, with nothing but the molten rock around them, Jerish spoke, "Everything we just went through was not real! Down to the very last detail, Axreal. It was all tricks and illusions!"

CreXan fell, exhausted, to the ground. Having ultimately failed, his elaborate ruse had drained him. Attempting to keep his body shielded, he tucked in his appendages and curled himself up into a ball like a roly-poly. Tucked completely inside of his hard glossy coating, he appeared like a giant purple steel ball with his foul odor enshrining him.

"Look, Axreal, now's the opportunity we've been waiting for," said Jerish.

"What do we do?" Axreal demanded.

"We will take him hostage. He has to have come from the Haven. So, he has to have a way back!" spoke Jerish. "We will make him take us to it, and we will shut The System down, once and for all!"

Axreal crouched to peer at the sickening ball of a creature. "Look

Jerish…without his lies and illusions, he is nothing!"

Jerish shouted at CreXan, "We know what the Lam Warons did to our world. You and your kind are to blame for our suffering. You had no right to do what you did! Tell me, where is your vessel?"

At first there came no reply. Jerish kicked at CreXan's shell. Then came a response.

"I will show you. Just do not injure me!" CreXan pleaded with the Setiacotions. *My grand illusion, in fine Lam Waron fashion*, he lamented, *you malformations would be in permanent comas by now, entering into your eternal rests laid out on the rock. Without me ever having to lift a talon! Your bones forever with the rest!*

"He appears to be in a weakened state, Jerish. But it may be another trick and it also may not last long," Axreal informed him.

"We are never going to fall for your tricks. You are nothing but a coward."

"Eeehhh, I the Great CreXan am not used to being treated in this fashion," CreXan squealed.

"We can arrange to treat you in a much worse way if you don't tell us where your ship is!" said Jerish.

"All right, okay. It is just beyond that large canyon. I had it set down into a crevice. Nearby is my capsule. You have to feel for it; it's invisible. You can board it and it will take you to my main ship."

"If you are lying, creature, I will ram this stone into your stinking body," Jerish did not like violence but knew he had to keep CreXan submissive.

Axreal spoke to Jerish, "We can roll his body over there. Maybe we should find a way to make sure he can't get away!"

"Okay. Go back to the ACS and bring all the fasteners you can find. Hurry. We have to tie him up!" Then Jerish spoke to CreXan, "Listen again, you creature. Don't attempt to do anything other than what we tell you. You are going to take us to the Haven. Let the other Lam Warons know not to try anything or you will be harmed!"

CreXan replied, "There are no others. I am the LAST!"

"Whul, that remains to be seen. We know you can't be trusted!" Jerish spoke as Axreal returned, "Hand me a fastener and let's get him tied up."

Once they finished tying him up, Axreal spoke, "Now, we need to feel for the capsule."

"We still need to watch him," said Jerish.

"Then we better find it quickly," said Axreal.

Jerish went one direction and Axreal went another. With arms outstretched, hands forward, and taking small steps, they moved forward, feeling all around them for the capsule.

"I found it!" yelled Axreal. "This is it. Come here. Feel this?"

"Oh yeah, you're right," said Jerish. Then he proceeded to kick up dirt, making a land marker. Jerish yelled towards CreXan, "Okay creature, how do we get in?"

"I have to speak commands to it. You will have to take me over to it," squealed the now-submissive CreXan.

Standing on one foot, Jerish and Axreal each raised one leg high and kicked, rolling CreXan forward.

At the capsule CreXan commanded, "Become visible, and let us enter."

Poking him once again, Jerish ordered CreXan, "Now, see to it that it takes us to your main ship. There you will direct it to transport us safely to the Haven."

Jerish and Axreal managed to position themselves for the brief ride aboard the capsule.

Axreal whispered so that, hopefully, only Jerish would hear. "We need to think about what we are going to do once we arrive at the Haven. Where are we supposed to go, and what we should do when we get there? Did Marshall tell you what to expect?"

"Whul no. We left for the quarries before he had much of a chance. I think he was waiting until we got back to tell us any details. It doesn't matter as much now. He," pointing at the huddled Lam Waron, "is going to tell us everything! Isn't that right, creature?"

"Yes," squealed CreXan. Then he thought to himself, *These insolent malformations actually believe I the Great, Marvelous, Supreme Baron have to do as they please! Well, they have another thing coming. All I need to do is access my portable system interface. That I can do once I am able to come out from here. I will notify Marlaxan and Petrexin of what is going on. They will come and help me put a stop to your little escapade. Nothing will interfere with Lam Waron operations. Least of all you two!*

The capsule swooped over the terrain and merged with *The Alustria*.

Once aboard Axreal remarked, "Look, Jerish, how impressive this is.

It is plush and comfortable. This is luxurious."

"Yeah, how many Setiacotions suffered to make it, huh creature? How many of the three species suffered and died for all of your things? Answer me?"

CreXan had to answer and proceed with caution. "I must command *The Alustria*. You want to get going now. Give me a moment to order it." CreXan then mustered the energy to command the ship, "TAKE ME TO THE HAVEN!"

"Answer me you stinking Lam Waron! How many suffered so you could have nice things?"

"We did everything for your good. We provided your people with full-time work, living accommodations, food, and, eeehhh, most of all we gave you purpose."

"You stole our planet. Polluted and raped it, and left her barely alive. You tricked them, like you tried to trick us. We were confined like prisoners. Food? You call that food? Those rations were horrible. You poisoned and controlled us and made us sick. We have seen the bodies buried outside the processing facilities. You will be made to pay for your crimes!"

"Come Jerish, I don't like to see you get this upset. You are going to make yourself sick thinking about it all. He is vile. We will set things right!"

CreXan felt the weight of his shell bare down on him. *It shouldn't be too much longer to the Resort, and maybe by that time I'll gain my strength and come back to full magnificence. They won't get far,* he thought.

The Alustria blasted through Eclipsia's outer atmosphere. The Resort Haven was a good thousand kilometers out, so they waited a long time until the Haven came into view on a projection above them.

"Incredible. Jerish, it is massive," Axreal could hardly believe her eyes.

The Resort Haven looked like a giant city laid out on an immense disk. Spires grouped together, making for a densely built-up center. Nestled below the disk stood all the internal workings that drove the Haven, including its lift-off engines. Attached above, clamped to the entire Haven was a redistributor ship. Its clawlike arms gripped the sides of the Haven. It helped bring the Haven out this far and stood ready for the relocation to Obscuria.

"This is where you live? Whul, the first thing you will do, creature, is to take us to where you control The System. You will make sure we get there safely! Anything goes wrong and I will be forced to end your life!"

"Are we going to have to roll him the entire way?" asked Axreal.

"Probably."

"My skid will be waiting to pick me up. We can ride it anywhere aboard I wish to go," squealed CreXan. The temperature inside his shell had become hot and sweltering. He would just have to wait till the right time to get free of it, if it was possible to break the restraints they had him in.

The Alustria entered the Haven. Its interior had been grand, but it did not compare with the grandiosity of the Resort Haven.

Jerish reveled in their victory at reaching this point, "We made it!"

Jerish and Axreal rolled CreXan out from *The Alustria*'s gangway while fighting their urge to gag the entire time.

"Alright. This must be the skid. Remember creature, there are to be no tricky moves by you, and you are to make sure The System leaves us alone. Do you understand?"

"Yes," came CreXan's lone reply.

The skid lowered to pick up CreXan, and Jerish and Axreal rolled him aboard.

"Take us to where you control The System! I have new orders for it."

With all of them aboard, they rode up and down numerous gaudy corridors. At one point they passed by Risase, who eagerly awaited her majesty's return home. She had received an alert, signaling *The Alustria*'s arrival. She frantically attempted to coordinate the drudges to prepare for their master's return. The Great Bath needed to be reconditioned and foods needed preparing. *He might want Gelaguise, or Citmop. Do we have any Chicgeza left? Or would he prefer a massage or mud treatment? Does he want music or gifts, or both?* She was overwhelmed. She was up to her eyeballs in confusion and her mind spun miserably.

The skid passed by her and she hadn't the clarity or sense to notice the appearance of the occupants aboard. In her mind, she saw CreXan as he always was. "I wonder where he is going. He didn't want to relax in his chambers first?"

She turned and hurried. The Kanda doorman failed to open the doors in enough time for her, and she smacked her mottled cheek into them, receiving a bruise.

"Ouch! His Greatness will just have to kiss me on my other cheek. Now, where did I see the kitchen?"

CreXan had ordered the skid to deliver them to a secret back door to his office. While in route he thought, *I can't let them have access to The System! I must somehow get out of here to address it.*

The heat inside his shell was becoming too much to bear, and he struggled to get out. He pressed his body outwards. With little in the way of give, he could not muster the strength needed to free himself. *This is bad, very bad.*

"Okay. We have come to a stop. Now tell us where we can control The System!"

"Eeeehhh, this should be my office. I can call the interface to descend. You will need my password. But I must be allowed to come out of here!"

"Jerish. We can't risk that."

"You will need to release me. There is no other way for it to work."

"You are trying to trick us," said Jerish.

"Is there any way we can let him out and still keep him restrained and under our control?" asked Axreal.

"Whul, I can wedge this rock into his flesh. A good gash should end his life. So he will obey us if he knows what is good for him."

"Let's go ahead and get in there," said Axreal.

CreXan had no need for a key. His presence was all the office's back door needed to open. With a swoosh, the door lifted upwards. Axreal and

Jerish rolled CreXan inside.

"We are going to release you," spoke Jerish. "If you make the slightest attempt to get away, this rock will be the last thing you'll ever feel."

They allowed CreXan to unfurl. Realizing instantly that his portable interface was no longer working, he panicked.

They watched in disgust as the Lam Waron's body came into closer view. The sight of his different-colored appendages, ending in long talons, shocked them. His pink and brown perspiration-covered nodules sickened them. The sight of his entire being along with his intensified odor caused Axreal to heave forward and release the contents of her stomach.

While keeping the rock firmly pressed against CreXan's neck with one hand, Jerish quickly pinched his nostrils shut with the other. With a muffled voice and crinkled brows, Jerish commanded, "Show us the interface!"

CreXan reluctantly called down the main interface. "Eeehhh, it will only respond with my password, and you must use your eyes and voice to direct it."

"Creature, give us the password now!"

"I refuse. You malformations haven't a clue who you are dealing with!"

Jerish drove the rock deeper, puncturing a vein. Pus spurted out of the rupture.

"We aren't playing any more games with you," replied Axreal. "Without access to the interface we do not need him alive. Just finish him!"

"Here it is. But you won't get very far," squealed CreXan, with the intention of accessing The System first. He recited, "Security comes from being in control." The first of the Lam Waron tenets.

"No, creature, security comes when you live in harmony with each other and the world!"

CreXan quickly attempted to address The System. He blasted, "System. Send emergency communiqué to Marlaxan and Petrexin: 'Operations compromised. Help!'" CreXan slipped out from under Jerish's threat. He scurried, making a "run" for the corridor.

"Jerish, he is getting away!"

"Let him go. We don't need him! System. Shut down all processing facilities and cease all activity."

"Cannot comply. Full sequence of passwords needed."

CreXan left a trail of dripping pus. He quickly located some Kanda outside of the office suite and gave them orders. Jerish and Axreal could hear CreXan's shrilling, "The Haven is under attack. Get in there and stop them now! Send my Kanda medics! I the greatest Lam Waron Baron cannot be allowed to remain injured. Hurry and get chief Kanda drudge Risase in here now. MOVE IT!"

Axreal spoke, "We need CreXan for the rest of the passwords."

Jerish spoke, "No. I have an idea. I'm going to try something else. Watch this."

"Be quick about it!"

"System, I need to give new instructions to all of the Setiacotions,

Remorans, and Kanda. Can that be done?"

"Affirmative. What are your instructions?"

"It's working!" exclaimed Axreal. She could hardly keep still.

Jerish triumphantly spoke, "Tell them: Free yourselves. Break out!"

The System instantly delivered Jerish's instructions to every Eclipsian slave. It stunned the Setiacotions, Remorans, and Kanda, stopping them in their tracks. The instructions confused them and they paused all their activities. Their sudden moment of self-awareness and idleness caused a major glitch in The System. It began to overload and back up.

Jerish had successfully duped The System!

Prison Break

The System responded, "System compromised. Due to species new instructions and momentary disengagement. System is experiencing mass resistance. Attempting to compensate."

"What does that mean?" asked Axreal.

"I think my message was received,"Jerish said. "The Setiacotions, Remoran, and Kanda are attempting to break free from the facilities!"

"If they are, they are having to fight The System. That means it's a battle!" said Axreal. "You know what else? I heard CreXan say something about the Kanda. The other species is *here,* Jerish, on the Haven."

"Whul, we've done what we set out to do. Marshall would be . . . proud! Now it will be up to them."

"Let's go see what's happening."

Chaos ensued everywhere. Thousands of Kanda had left their posts.

The corridors were filled with the clatter and commotion of thousands of madly dashing Kanda, each looking for an escape. They scuttled about like Chicgeza in a maze with no way out. Shouts could be heard over the ruckus: "How do we get free?" "Where's the way out?" "We need to go this way!" "Don't go there!"

CreXan also witnessed the mayhem. He blasted into the crowding Kanda, "Why aren't you all working? Get back to your duties!" His words had no effect. He felt shock as he saw all of the Kanda involved in a mutiny. When he caught sight of Risase he called out to her, "Risase, my dear, attend to me. I need medical assistance!"

Risase replied, "I'm . . . I'm busy . . . freeing myself . . . and breaking out! Do you know where the exit is?" When CreXan did not answer immediately, Risase rejoined with the crowd and was not seen again.

Brought down and humiliated, CreXan spoke, "Ooohhh . . . Damn!" He had lost all control. His power and wealth were escaping him. "They all have been turned against me and The System." Next he realized, *The other Barons will be on the way. Eeehhh, when they see what has gone on here, they will liquefy me! It's those infernal malformations. I've got to get away. They will harm me.* His only option now was to blend in, disguise himself as a Kanda, and maybe worm his way to *The Alustria*.

The effects of the incorporated three species' disengagement from The System soon became apparent on the Resort Haven. One thing after another went wrong. Soon havoc prevailed. The Resort Haven swung and the simulated gravity fluctuated slightly, sending the Kanda jostling to from one side to the other. The illumination flickered as the power could no longer be consistently maintained. The giant clamps of the redistributor ship lost their hold and the Resort Haven detached, losing its orbit and plummeted toward Eclipsia.

The rapid descent of the Haven put a great burden on its internal support structures. As stress built up, walls began to shift and buckle, fires broke out, and the Resort Haven's contents flung madly about.

Inside CreXan's suite, glass littered the floors from a multitude of shattered mirrors. Curtains dropped from perches above, furniture fell over, and cracks spread across the walls. Water from the Great Bath had spilled out and flowed everywhere. Linens, platters, and garments dropped out from storage spaces. Exposed wiring set fire to CreXan's hand crafted carpet, which depicted the Serendipity. The fire quickly spread to his life-size replica and turned it to ash.

The Kanda yelled and screamed as some suffered injuries. A large piece of artwork fell, crushing and pinning a Kanda beneath it. Numerous Kanda gasped as the air pressure changed. A Kanda drudge fell over a railing, having been knocked from a third tier landing in the great atrium, and plummeted screaming to her death.

CreXan struggled to make his way unaided through the smoke-filled chambers, in the shifting gravity, and without his skid. As a Kanda, his struggle was somewhat easier, but he was not accustomed to having to do so much for himself. *He* tired.

"Somehow I have got to get to *The Alustria*," CreXan coughed. He pressed his outstretched Kanda hands against the exterior walls of the encyclopedia vault to steady himself.

Then from out of nowhere, a sallow-looking Kanda female approached him. Her tattered and dirty textured dress was of a refined type, usually associated with CreXan's closest Kanda drudges. She had a fire in her eyes, which was not a reflection of the surrounding inferno.

"You can't hide from *me*!" yelled Lorese, no longer confined to her quarters. She carried a piece of broken glass in one hand, while madly cramming down rations with the other.

"Oh, no!" CreXan shook with fear. "Not you!" Looking at the glass shard in her hand he squealed, "You wouldn't!"

"O Great and Wonderful CreXan, *yes,* I would! You see I have nothing to lose and so much satisfaction to gain! They all seem to think there is a way out of here. Whatever made them think that? You and I know there isn't one for them. And I'm going to make sure you don't get out of here either!" She began to laugh uproariously. Lorese, with her bones protruding, and one arm raised, charged at him. She slashed at his face, leaving several gashes.

CreXan, reeling from pain, struggled to initiate Lorese's chem-pac in order to destroy her. Luckily for her, it had quit functioning while she starved in her quarters. When his attempt to destroy her failed, he desperately tried to slither past her.

The irate and renourished Lorese screamed, "Die, you worm! Die!" She let loose the shard, sending it into his belly.

No longer able to retain the illusion of being a Kanda, CreXan retook his Lam Waron appearance.

The shard made a small but deep cut. Acid shot out from his stomach and hit Lorese in the eyes.

"Aaahhh!" Lorese screamed in anguish. "I can't see!"

CreXan seized the opportunity to flee. As his wounds began to crust over, he quickly fled for *The Alustria*.

Lorese, still struggling to see, dashed through the smoky, crowded, and noise-filled corridors in search of CreXan. "I'll kill you or die trying. I don't even care if I catch on fire to do it!" she yelled after him.

CreXan, filled with fumes and bruising defeat, barely could hold himself together. With Lorese far behind and still searching for him, he said, "What is wrong with me. How could I have lost control?" CreXan did not even recognize himself. He scurried along, arriving at the chamber that held *The Alustria*. Once situated aboard he ordered, "Take me far away from here!" He mistakenly assumed he still had an ounce of authority.

The chamber outside erupted in flame and enveloped *The Alustria*. It blew apart, incinerating its passenger.

Jerish and Axreal ducked into a corner and barely managed to avoid being trampled by the incited Kanda.

"Grasp my hand," spoke Jerish. "We are going to need to stay close to each other or we'll get separated or lost."

"It feels like we are falling Jerish. This whole place is going to crash into our planet!"

"There's no way through all this."

"I don't want to crash to my death!" said Axreal.

"Whul, we don't have another choice other than to ride the Haven down. Maybe we can breach before it impacts," said Jerish.

"I'm scared Jerish."

"Yeah, me too."

Axreal spoke, "Hold me tight."

"We will be alright. As long as we stay together, I know we will be fine. We need to get to an upper level!"

Ignoring the mayhem, Jerish and Axreal saw what The System was desperately attempting to do to regain control.

"It's The System again!" said Axreal as she stared ahead wide-eyed."

The System attempted to apprehend the Kanda. It released hundreds of giant, crimson balloons, system macrophages. The inflating macrophages tried to surrounded each of the Kanda. Only some of the macrophages succeeded in capturing the Kanda. The ones they captured ended up suffocating as the macrophages inflated tightly around them. The macrophages could not keep up with the sheer number of loose Kanda. There simply were not enough of them. This, The System's last attempt at control aboard the Haven failed miserably.

The macrophages began to pop and burst from the ensuing destruction, leaving suffocated Kanda in their wake.

Just then Jerish looked up. "Watch out!" he yelled. A portion of the vaulted ceiling came crashing down. It just barely missed hitting them. "Whew, that was close!"

Vibrations shook the Haven. The noise was almost enough to rupture

Jerish's and Axreal's eardrums.

"This looks about as far as we go," Jerish yelled over the volume. "There is no way further. We have to wait it out here!"

They had, in fact, made it to one of the larger spires in that particular section. Suddenly emergency doors confined them to a small, cramped room.

"You look . . ." said Axreal while crouching down, "a lot like when I first met you." She rubbed her finger gently above his brows to remove a streak of soot and grime from his forehead.

"If anything happens, Axreal, I want you to know this has been the most incredible time. I thank Auria Isis for bringing us together. I know we made a difference, Axreal! We took on The System and the Lam Waron! No matter what happens now we gave our people a chance for better!"

"You're right no matter what happens, Jerish, being together made for an incredible experience. You are my best friend . . . If it weren't for you . . ."

"Whul now, we succeeded *together* . . ."

More emergency doors closed down throughout the Resort. They acted to preserve normal air pressure and to prevent fires from spreading. They also locked everyone in, tightly packed, as the Haven fell smack towards Eclipsia's surface.

Meantime, on the planet's surface, confrontation and hostility broke out at all Eclipsian processing facilities. Explosions, fires, and conflicts erupted as The System waged an all-out assault against the escaping Setiacotions and Remorans.

The Setiacotions and Remorans strove to carry out their new programming. In doing so, they had to fight for their lives against the attacking System. Many thousands became entangled in the violence and were injured. Some succumbed to the onslaught of the bioengineered gasses. Others could not find a way out of their podules. Without The System's clear instructions, some podules smashed into each other, as others began piling up in the connectways. Plantech 4, a large food-procurement facility, flooded with bioaltering gasses and macrophages. Thousands died seeking a way out. Plantech 200 filled with plodropeds. The incited plodropeds ripped and tore through flesh, splattering much in the way of Setiacotion and Remoran blood. Several dockyard towers gave way, reducing everything beneath to rubble. In all, two billion Setiacotion and Remoran slaves sought to free themselves and to break out from their miserable incorporation.

The System became overwhelmed in the conflict. It fought to maintain some semblance of control and authority. However, messages began flooding its central control hub, and The System could not keep up. It soon overloaded. Its last message registered at CreXan's interface: "SYSTEM CORRUPTED, SHUTDOWN DUE TO THERMAL EVENT." The hub blew up, taking The System with it.

With no one in command, the Setiacotions and Remorans had to fight off the last remnants of The System's assault. Some had taken up tools to cut their way through, some found weapons slated for sale to the consumer worlds. These they also used to clear their path to freedom. Setiacotions had also been successful in plugging gas vents and stopping the dispersal of the plodropeds.

With the impenetrable wall barrier destroyed, Setiacotions and Remorans were gradually making their way out onto the surface. Thousands of sick, confused, and wounded Setiacotions and Remorans began maneuvering their strange new surroundings. On the outskirts of the ravaged processing facilities, Setiacotion and Remorans began to collect and form into survivor groups.

Destruction completely leveled certain processing facilities, and none survived at those. There, radioactivity was released and took the form of matter, time, and space distortions. These cloudlike masses of radiation quickly became airborne and dispersed.

Outlying facilities integrated with the Eclipsian system, soon turned into complete uproar and chaos. Setiacotions trapped on Urxis Minor suffocated to death. When the ceilings blew off the mining operations on the nonatmospheric asteroid, the slaves became fair game to the ravages of space.

Left without communication, the Obscurian processing facilities fell into disorder and chaos. The singular incorporated species at the Obscurian facilities reverted to their prior condition and they, too, sought to break free from their captivity.

Dimatian buyers, who were en route for scheduled meetings with CreXan aboard their government ship, halted when they discovered problems during their approach vector.

Lam Waron conglomerates had provided them, and certain other consumer-world elite, with ships capable of bringing them to remote places like Eclipsia. This provided carefully monitored and controlled access to a select few. In that way they could attend meetings and carry on business in secret. The ships' computers kept the routes and locations confidential.

"Better come up and take a look," the pilot of the Dimatian government ship called to his passengers. Two Dimatian officials, "buyers," in business attire, came up to the command deck. "I am not getting any signal from Lam Waron Conglomerates. We are usually greeted and granted clearance at this point," said the pilot. "I am getting strange readings, mixed, and all across the board. It looks like there's been some sort of incident."

One official buyer spoke. "We must be able to place our orders. Can't you get a signal through to the Baron! We can't be delayed; our meeting is scheduled to begin."

The pilot spoke. "I am trying sir. There doesn't seem to be anyone home."

The other official joined in. "Perhaps you can get us in a little *closer*. Maybe when they see that it is us, they will respond and give us the coordinates to get us aboard."

"I'll see if I can take us in closer. They usually won't let you approach even as close as we are now! I am afraid, officials, that something terrible may have happened."

The Dimatian pilot was astounded that full clearance seemed to have been given to them, even without word having been sent. He was able to fly the massive government ship ever closer to the planet. It skimmed over the surface. The destruction soon became apparent. Smoldering facilities burned across the horizon, plumes of soot towered over the land, and what appeared to be the workers were gathering outside.

"What has happened here?" replied the official buyers in unison.

"It has all been destroyed," spoke the pilot.

"Pilot, take us out of here. We have to report this immediately. They'll want an investigation out here. We are in no position to do that," said one official.

The other spoke. "Send word, just in case, to CreXan, 'Your Graciousness, looks like we will need to reschedule. We will await your communiqué.'"

"Get us back on route to Dimatia. I'll need to talk to Chief Liaison Vorsh at once!"

Meantime, portions of the gigantic Resort Haven began to splinter as its massive bulk tore into the murky atmosphere. Its great superstructure started to separate from its inner compartments. Trails of gas and fumes followed behind huge chunks of falling debris. Within could be seen the Kanda caught by surprise as walls, floors, and roofing lifted off and separated from all around them. They went freefalling towards impact with the surface. Other sections broiled in flames.

"When I say 'Breach,' we head straight up and come out clear from the top of the Haven," Jerish yelled to Axreal.

Both sat a pace apart, eyes squeezed shut, and with their particular chamber still intact. Axreal's ringlets flew about wildly. Soot, sweat, fear, and gold ceiling flakes covered them.

"How will you know it's the right time?" asked Axreal.

"Trust me. I'll know."

The gaudy spire chamber they rode in came close to impact.

"Breach!" yelled Jerish.

It began. A hundred thousand vibrations for Axreal. A hundred thousand revolutions for Jerish. They blurred into the background. Left behind, afterimages. Ghosts. Vanishment. Successful breaches.

Both breached, coming partially out to assess whether they were each free of the Haven and its destructive aftermath. Then they breached back downward, avoiding impact.

"We did it!" Axreal said ecstatically.

"Whul . . . sounds like you had doubts," prodded Jerish.

"Well, I never had any before. Now I won't ever again."

"Oh, so you did doubt me?"

"I did not say that. You can't say I said that."

"Okay, Axreal, you're right. Anyways, we need to get clear of here."

"Let's find the survivors."

The Resort Haven lay scattered in millions of pieces, across an Eclipsian wasteland. Amongst the smoldering wreck, a few survivors emerged. Jerish and Axreal watched as the Kanda began to gather.

"They don't have any idea where they are, or what to do next. Some are badly hurt, and those didn't make it," Axreal said, pointing to some of the crash victims. "What about the injured?" asked Axreal, feeling a pang in her heart.

"I don't know. Whul, maybe some of the Kanda will know what to do."

"Let's get their attention, talk to them, and find out what can be done," said Axreal.

"Here, I know what to do," Jerish proceeded to climb onto some wreckage. The sheet of metal clanked and swayed with his weight. He balanced on it, making a platform from which to draw the Kanda's attention. "Everyone listen! Please! You need to listen! Come closer. We have got to get together. Do any of you know how to care for the injured? Also, we need to see if there are any supplies—food and rations, coverings—in the wreckage."

A host of replies came from the Kanda. Some thought they might have the means to tend to the wounded. Others had ideas where they could obtain supplies.

"I was one of CreXan's medics!" replied a male. "Well, for numerous people…we need to set up a large area to start treating the wounded. I'll need a lot of help though, setting up, moving them, prioritizing . . . "

"Great!" spoke Jerish, "You, you, and you over there, start setting up a place here for the injured. We'll need shelters. Those that are strongest need to locate the wounded and assist with bringing them back. If any are found uninjured, we need to enlist their help." Jerish assembled groups to begin sifting through what was left of the Haven for supplies and necessities, "Everyone over here needs to start looking for things we can use. Be on the lookout for drinking water, medical supplies, food, and anything to cover up with," he told them. Then he turned to Axreal, "We are going to have to try to survive here, at least for a while. There is no telling how far away the quarries are," said Jerish. "We will eventually need to move them there."

"How can the quarries provide for all these people?"

"Whul, they can't. At least not now. But it is their main chance for survival."

"I am going to go see what help I can be to the medic," replied Axreal. "Hopefully, this will soon be over and the Kanda will recover!"

"Yeah! I am on my way now. There's a lot we are going to need. I've got to keep the Kanda organized. I'll meet up with you after a while!"

Later, as Talrish started to descend and night approached, much had been accomplished outside the crashed Haven on the Eclipsian wasteland. Kandas had erected shelters and gathered supplies. The Kanda had located some tanks that held uncontaminated water. So they did have water reserves.

CreXan's former medics, along with Axreal, tended to the burn victims. Sadly, many injured Kanda remained beyond help. And they had to leave many where they had fallen. The destruction of the Resort Haven had freed many from their misery.

"It will be dark soon, Jerish," said Axreal. "We are tired. There's not much more we can do until tomorrow. Here, these aren't great, but it will fill you up," Axreal said while handing Jerish some of the Kanda's artificial rations, which they had luckily recovered.

"Whul, these taste awful. But you are right. They stave off some of my hunger."

"Have a good rest, Jer, and I will see you in the morning."

"You too. You've never called me that before."

"It fits somehow now. Don't you think?"

"Sure. Whatever you think is fine by me."

Jerish and Axreal got as comfortable as they could and eventually fell asleep.

Jerish fell into a deep slumber. While in the deepest part of his sleep, he dreamed. She sang once again to him.

For so long have I waited, all can be as it once was. All is within your grasp; all can be as it was meant. Freedom, Joy, and Harmony can return. For my children are set free and returning. What was once can be again.

"Auria Isis?"

"Yes, child. I have come to thank you, as I am also doing for Axreal. You both have helped set things back to being right. So many great things will happen in your remaining days. It is because of you that there are no more prisons, which confine my children. They can come back to living in harmony with me. I am getting better. Repairs can be made. Now my long, painful waiting is over. My children are free!"

"I will continue to do whatever I need to do, to see that things are set back right."

"I am grateful. My dear Jerish, I am so very grateful."

Axreal dreamed, and within that dream, Auria Isis came to her, singing.

For so long have I waited, all can be as it once was. All is within your grasp; all can be as it was meant. Freedom, Joy, and Harmony can return. For my children are set free and returning. What was once can be again.

"Auria Isis?"

"Yes, child. I have come to thank you, as I am also doing for Jerish. You both have helped set things back to being right. It is because of your compassion and undergoing peril that things have been put back right. The darkness is lifting. My children are free!"

"How are we going to make it back to the quarries? How are all of us going to survive? How are we going to clean up all this mess someday?"

"So many questions, dear child. Do not worry. For now, you need your rest. As surely as there will be a tomorrow, the answers will come."

Far and beyond, wondrous realities lie ahead for you, and for all. You'll achieve more than you can possibly know . . .

The Return to Dignity

The quarries bore witness to the recent upheaval at the processing facilities. The gel creatures had watched as smoke and soot moved above the rooftop membranes along with floating distortions of radiation.

Meantime, the gel creatures eagerly awaited the six Setiacotions emergence from the tubular plants. As upheaval raged over most of Eclipsia, the six Setiacotions, safely encased in their "walnut" cocoons underwent their miraculous metamorphosis.

Kurby, on the other hand, astounded Torbot's people with what he was undergoing. After his time spent amongst the comfort of the quarries, Kurby began to experience a profound change. At first he noticed an aching pain, which soon covered his entire unsymmetrical body.

The gel creatures watched in shock as Kurby began to separate.

Remorans were composite beings. They consisted of multiple organisms that in times of hardship, undue stress, and at birth would join to form one being. They could group together and meld entirely to become one total being. When the original Lam Waron Harvesters had begun to apprehend them from the surface, the individuals united to form single beings. The trauma within The System never allowed them to separate. Kurby actually was comprised of six separate Remorans who were born together as one for mutual safety and survival. "Kurby" was the sum of individual beings.

Experiencing natural food and being within the harmony and warmth of the quarries allowed for this profound change in Kurby. The six separated out from the whole. There were now six spongelike Remorans.

The gel creatures did not expect such a dramatic change. There had been no record of this Remoran characteristic or ability. It made them wonder all the more as to what may result from the Setiacotions now awaiting their transformations.

Sallus, a colony botanist, had been doing much in the way of inscribing notations. She had witnessed the disjoining of Kurby, among other things. One morning while surveying the newly carved-out sections, she made a discovery.

Amazing. What is this? They've grown overnight. Sallus imparted outward so that anyone close by would receive her impartation, though there were none. She had discovered a patch of extended and accelerated growth. She parted the foliage. Then she used several of her arms to sift through the soil where she had noticed something odd sticking out. *What is this? A new plant?* She glided back to make her discovery known. She popped through an oval opening at the colony. Inside, she quickly imparted, *Take notice. It seems things are expanding faster than we thought. There is extensive growth out in the newly carved sections today. If this keeps up, in no time there will be enough food here to provide for hundreds of Setiacotions and Remorans. I found something you all need to see. There is something new growing.*

A group of gel creatures sprang to the site. In just the time since Sallus had been gone more growth had occurred. One of the elder gel creatures surveyed the site and messaged to the assemblage, *Observe. Our diligence and long-held efforts have been rewarded again. Life is expanding. Along with the Setiacotions' and Remorans' return, there has been exponential growth. Things are coming back . . . my fellow people . . . Eclipsia is reawakening.*

Epilogue: Reckoning on the Consumer World Dimatia

Ordus said nervously, "We can't tell them what has happened." He could not keep what he knew from making every cell in his body quiver.

"They will find out soon enough," replied Vorsh.

"There will be chaos and pandemonium if we do," Ordus said.

The vast, colorful marketplace of Tatamum Square held thousands of passerbys. Its advertising banners blew in the breeze. Mothers with nurslings at their sides and providers getting off from shifts at work hurried away to take foodstuffs, care of Lam Waron Conglomerates, home for the evening meal. Others, including a few alien races, shopped the vast mall.

"In a week or two the news will hit anyways. We should have done something about it long ago. Now there is nothing we can do," spoke

Vorsh.

Vorsh had been appointed Chief Liaison of Foreign Trade Affairs for Dimatia by his old university buddy, President Wersh. He gladly accepted the appointment a number of years ago at President Wersh's encouragement.

"Vorsh," President Wersh had told him. "It is a veritable stroll in the park. Our business with the Lam Warons is the best thing that ever happened. We can get everything we need for little cost. Everything is already set up. There's really nothing to this job. Except a big fat pay voucher."

Vorsh could not refuse the offer. Most of the time, all he had to do was attend government parties and meetings. He had visited some of the Lam Waron manufacturing worlds, even met with that CreXan fella a few times.

"I should have looked into things more!" spoke Vorsh, now equally traumatized by the impact of the situation. "Everything was made to look fine on the surface."

"You could not have known. Don't beat yourself up about it. None of us knew," spoke Ordus.

"That isn't true. You heard the rumors, we all did. We did nothing about it, we did nothing," tears fell from Vorsh's convex humanoid eyes. "Year after year we went on as if nothing were wrong. Well, something was terribly wrong."

"I know. I have seen the report from your office," said Ordus.

Word had reached Vice President Ordus at his office at 101 Tatamum

Spiral Towers. He had watched the visual report. It relayed that battery shipments had not shown as per schedule. Dimatia imported all its energy from Lam Waron Conglomerates. The batteries fueled their entire society. Without them, everything would come to a halt. The report had gone on to show an investigation which revealed that Lam Waron Conglomerates had suffered a major shutdown out on Eclipsia and its other surrounding facilities. Pictures had come back showing the terrible destruction. Millions of tortured slaves had rioted and broken out from their cruel captivity. Some managed to survive. Most did not. The processing facilities had gone up in flames. Giant explosions had leveled many of them. Three species of wounded, burned, and sick victims badly needed help.

"Our reports here show, Vice President, that orders for food, clothing, merchandise, and fuel have not been showing for about a month. In fact, nothing has shown up at all for the last few days. We can't go on for very long without supplies. When the citizenry finds out, they'll come to me looking for answers. Ordus, they are going to kill me," Vorsh said.

"Is there *anywhere* else we can get back up fuel and batteries and food? What about Travis Suppliers?" asked Ordus.

Vorsh shook his head, "They haven't been in business for years. The fact is, Ordus, we make nothing of our own. We produce nothing for ourselves and have lost the know-how. Everything got moved off-world decades ago."

"It is time I let President Wersh know. Perhaps we should get out of here. That," Ordus said as he motioned toward the crowd, "is a lot of people that will turn real angry here real fast."

"That is a lot of families that won't be able to feed their children," replied Vorsh.

Just then, the mall's lamps flickered and went dark. Panic erupted from the crowd.

"It is already happening. Quickly! We must get to President Wersh," stated Ordus adamantly.

"You do whatever you want. Take this as my formal resignation. I have a family of my own to take care of. I am out of here," said the now Ex-Chief of Trade Vorsh.

"Vorsh!" Ordus called after him.

Vorsh made his way to a subterrain vehicle. Luckily, the car had fuel to get him home to the out-cities. *I have got to get home and get Helia and the nurslings out to the glades.*

When Vorsh arrived to his families plat, he hurried through the entry flap where he was met by his son. Helia would be taking care of their two nurslings and getting a meal ready for all.

"Dearest Jerish, not now," Vorsh refused his son the customary rhythmic hand greeting.

"What is it, provider? What is wrong?" the Dimatian youth had never seen his father in such a state before.

"Helia!" Vorsh yelled, "Get the nurslings! We need to pack all the foodstuffs, batteries, water, illuminators, extra clothes. Jerish, get upstairs and start packing your essentials. You will have to leave behind your motorized minicar."

It was from Vorsh's son that Jerish from Eclipsia had taken his name. It was the Dimatian youth's fancy present that the Setiacotion had witnessed being manufactured at the processing facilities some time ago. It was on the present's tag that Jerish from Eclipsia found his name.

"In the name of the divine," worried Helia, "What is going on, Vorsh?"

"We have got to get out of the out-city now and to the glade home. It will be safer there!"

"Safer? Safer from what?" replied Helia.

"Provider," Jerish, the Dimatian youth, asked his mother, "is my father provider alright?"

"Oh yes, youngster. Let me talk to him alone," Helia's dark emerald eyes opened wide with concern as she addressed her mate out of her children's earshot. "Calm down Vorsh. I am sure whatever it is, we can work it out together."

"Mate, you don't understand," Vorsh let the dam gates flood. "It is the end of our civilization, Helia. We based everything entirely on importing off-world goods. We relied entirely on the wrong things. Not having to make anything for ourselves seemed like the best possible plan to free up our people for other endeavors. We didn't look deep enough into how those goods were being made. Now we know. Did you ever hear the name *Eclipsia* mentioned before?"

"Yes. I think so. It was a long time ago. It's some sort of factory, I believe," Helia did her best to recall.

"It was where almost all of our goods have been coming from. It was a large manufacturing world run by Lam Waron Conglomerates out beyond Ashton's Belt, or some backwater place like that. They had captured slaves there and imprisoned them. They had been torturing and poisoning them for eons. Now that the slaves have fortunately gotten free, they have rioted. The bad news is, the factories on Eclipsia are no longer producing our food, supplies . . . Dimatia is going to run out of everything. We maybe have a few days, a week, before anarchy strikes."

"This is horrible. It explains why shelves have been empty lately," spoke Helia, "I'll, I'll get packing." Helia, frazzled by the shocking news, scrambled to empty the foodstuffs. Damn those Lam Warons, *I never did like that evil company very much. Damn you to the cleansing fires!*

We hope you enjoyed our novel. Be sure and look for the sequel which is currently in the works.

www.ingramcontent.com/pod-product-compliance
Lightning Source LLC
Chambersburg PA
CBHW032028240626
47154CB00003B/829